SEX
LOVE
REPEAT

ALESSANDRA TORRE

Select Publishing LLC
Miramar Beach, Florida 32550
alessandratorre.com

Printed in the United States of America

First paperback edition: December 2013

Cover Design: Miguel Kilantang Jr - mizworks.com

Editor: Madison Seidler – MadisonSeidler.com

Library of Congress Cataloging-in-Publication Data

Other Books by Alessandra Torre:
Blindfolded Innocence
The Diary of Brad De Luca
Masked Innocence (Feb 2014)
The End of the Innocence (Mar 2014)
The Girl in 6E
The Dumont Diaries

This book is for the girl with her head down,
and the inner strength I know she carries.

The heart is stubborn. It holds onto love despite what sense and emotion tells it. And it is often, in the battle of those three, the most brilliant of all.

"Madison."

I hear my name, but I cannot open my eyes. I try, pushing and pulling with the weak muscles of my eyelids, but there is no movement. Nothing to minimize the blackness, nothing to pull me from this rabbit hole of darkness. But I can hear. I have emerged into awareness with only one sense, and I grab onto it and pull upward, trying to raise myself into life through the elements of sound alone. I heard my name, heard Paul say it, crystal clear, his voice thick with emotion. I strain for more, worried he has left, tensing and pushing every muscle I have, trying for movement, trying to reach out with my hands and grab his skin, his shirt, anything.

Then I pause on my journey, all my efforts freezing, stalled in their worthless attempts, because a second voice has joined the first.

Stewart.

A voice I love—his deep, authoritative tone one that traditionally makes my breath quicken and my knees weak. But here, in this place, it makes my heart drop. His voice should never be heard in tandem with Paul's, their presences should never be intersected, much less raised in what sounds to be an argument.

And I know, as my mind closes off—pushes me deeper into the black rabbit hole of oblivion, my subconscious fighting tooth and nail as I am pulled down, down, down—I have failed. All of my attempts, my careful lives of separation …

"Madison." I hear my name one last time, but it is so faint, I cannot tell which man it comes from.

THREE MONTHS EARLIER

DANA

I am nosy. A meddler. Mom used to say it would be my downfall. She was probably right. It certainly got me in enough trouble early in life, my matchmaking skills often falling flat, my snooping ending disastrously. As an adult, I should know better. I should keep to myself—keep my curiosity to a minimum.

I haven't seen Stewart in two years. Ever since we had a big blow up over Thanksgiving dinner and his inability to have time for anything but work. I now regret that fight. It was valid, and I was in the right, but it wasn't worth the silence. Silence that stretched a week, then a month, then years, each passing holiday a reminder of my loss. I don't know if it's his stubbornness or the fact that his busy schedule has pushed thoughts of me out of his mind. I don't know what's worse—intentionally being snubbed or being forgotten about completely.

For me, it was initially stubbornness, our commonalities peaking in that one trait: pride. And since I, after all, was right, there was really no reason for me to break first—to weaken and reach out when he was the one in error. Now, it doesn't really matter whether I was right. I just want him back. Sadly, my point has been proven even more by his silence. He doesn't have time for me. He only has time for work. And for her. That blonde who holds his busy heart in her hands.

I first saw them in the society pages, his hand tight around her waist, her smile bright and natural, affection in her eyes as she beamed at him. He is so rarely photographed, never having the time for the premieres or charity galas that most men of his position flock to like obedient animals. He doesn't lunch at the Ivy or stroll through Beverly Hills. He takes the elevator down from his condo, walks four buildings west, and rides a different elevator up to his office. Work. Sleep. Repeat. At least that was his life when I knew it. When I had a part, however small, in his heart. Maybe things are different now. Maybe he takes weekends off, has dinner dates, movie nights, and tropical vacations, and takes that ray of California blonde right along with him.

But I doubt it. My online stalking has shown no such habits. Best I can tell, he is the same Stewart—*she* is the only change.

Whether she is a passing fancy or a long-term possibility, that is yet to be known. I will find out. I moved here, in small part, to become a part of his life again. Whether he wants me to or not. So I'll find out more about her. I'll know soon enough how much of a role she plays in his life. I'll sit back, watch, and gather information. He is certainly too busy to notice my eyes.

MADISON

I don't know what it is about a wealthy man that women find appealing, but I am victim to it along with the rest of society. And Stewart wears wealth as well as any man I know.

The backdrop of finery complements him, his large frame settling into expensive leather chairs; crystal chandeliers often cast dramatic lighting that highlights the beautiful lines of his face, and brilliant blue of his eyes. His Philipe Patek watch glints, the edge of it barely visible under the cuff of his dress shirts. His custom suits move easily beneath my fingers, sliding over his broad shoulders, the hard definition of trained muscles rippling under pale skin. His skin never sees the light of day, his hours spent indoors, his workouts done under the muted lights of his penthouse gym and directed by a blonde bombshell named Tiffany. We have fucked on the rubber mat in that gym, my back bare against the soft floor, his shorts yanked down enough for his cock to pull out, his intensity extra beautiful under the glow of gentle lights and a sheen of sweat on his bare chest.

Tonight, I only have to step inside, my entrance interrupting a set of pull-ups, his muscles popping as he suspends and lifts himself with easy efficiency. The additional light of the open door causes them both to turn, his eyes locking on mine with laser focus, and he drops lightly to his feet. "Tiffany," he says between hard breaths. "That'll be all."

I drop my bag as she hurries past, barely noticing the sound of her exit, my focus on Stewart, as he strides forward and grips my arms, lifting me easily and silently onto the counter, his lips pressing against mine quickly, before interrupting us with the cloth of my shirt, pulling it over my head and tossing it aside. He skips a greeting, focusing on my bare breasts, pressing me backward and taking a hungry mouth to my skin, his hands yanking and pulling on my shorts, sliding them down and off of my legs as his tongue plays a soft rhythm against my nipple.

He moves lower, tasting me, inhaling deeply between my legs. "God Madison, you taste so good." He groans against my sex, his tongue dipping inside and fucking me thickly, his need pouring through his mouth and his hands, which ravage my body like I am their final meal to feast on. They curl under me, lifting, and he carries me to the bench and lays me down, his eyes dark and wild as he stares down at me, pulling down the cloth of his shorts until his cock pops free.

"This," he murmurs, "is going to be for me. I promise, I'll take care of you later."

I smile, spreading my legs apart and stretching out on the bench. His brand of fucking is relentless, strong fucks in which he devours my body without restraint. It is what I have come here for—it is what I want. I need the domination, the edge of insanity that he barely holds in check. I need the madness in his eyes, the pure need that breathes through his body, the need only I can satisfy.

And there, on the leather bench, he rides us both to exhaustion.

I wake in his bed, two sheets between me and the down comforter, the soft voice of Estelle somewhere to my right. I roll over, blinking sleepily as her kind face comes into view.

"Are you ready for breakfast Ms. Madison?"

"What time is it?" I prop myself up, holding the blanket against my bare chest.

"It's after ten, ma'am. Mr. Brand told me to wake you after—"

I nod, smiling slightly. "Yes. I didn't mean to sleep this long. What time did he leave?"

"Six-thirty ma'am."

I look around for my clothes, trying to trace back the moment when they had become victim to Stewart's hands. *His office.* "I asked you a year ago to stop calling me ma'am," I mumble, a yawn slipping out of my mouth.

"Yes, ma'am." She frowns regretfully, before starting over. "I'm sorry. I mean Madison. Would you care for breakfast?"

"No, thank you. I've got to get going. My clothes from yesterday—"

"Were in the office. They have been gathered and are in the laundry room. I will make sure they are hung in your closet once clean."

"Perfect. Thank you. Do you mind asking the valet to bring up my car?"

"Certainly. I'll be close by if you need me." She smiles brightly before backing into the hall and closing the suite's doors.

Almost ten. I yawn again, blinking the sleep from my eyes, and slide from the bed. I walk into the granite-filled bathroom and turn on the steam shower.

VENICE BEACH, CA

I step from the bedroom a half hour later, jeans and a tank top on, my wet hair twisted into a bun. I swing by the kitchen on my way out, waving goodbye to Estelle and snagging a red apple and bottled water from the fridge.

I hop on Santa Monica Boulevard, moving through lanes of traffic with ease, my car knowing the route as well as my soul, my thoughts wandering as I drive. My Audi was a gift from Stewart, my twenty-ninth birthday present, probably picked out by his assistant. Regardless of who chose the vehicle, I love it. White exterior, blood red leather inside, it is sleek, sexy, and just begs every degenerate in my neighborhood to steal it. I am shocked it has survived for the last five months.

It's fourteen miles between Stewart's home and mine, but it might as well be different countries. Stewart lives in the fast-paced world of downtown Hollywood, rarely leaving the blocks of the city unless jetting off for work. He doesn't own a plane; he doesn't spend his money on much other than his home, his clothes, and me. He doesn't have time to spend money and doesn't believe in purchasing things just because he can. He works a hundred hours a week, sleeps six hours a night, and fucks the hell out of me the rest of the time. His needs are minimum: food, sleep, and sex. I take care of one of those. Estelle and his bed take care of the rest.

I get off on Lincoln Boulevard, the traffic lessening, frustrated drivers continuing their zip along the freeway, anxious to continue their painful life. I wish, for a brief moment, that I had put down the car's top, needing the wind in my hair and the sound of the surf. Leaving Stewart's, I sometimes need the wash of fresh air. A strong breeze to release the intensity he carries with him.

I pull off the road, turning down our street. Pressing the garage release button, I enter the dark space that is my spot and kill the ignition. I step out in dim light, the overhead burnt out, Paul promising for the last five months to get around to it.

The steps are worn concrete, this townhome complex built before developers knew what they had, before they realized that this close to the beach they shouldn't build shit housing. Back before property values hit ridiculous figures, and a six-figure income still puts you in the projects, dodging street beggars and used needles. We don't make six-figures. Paul brings in anywhere from fifty to sixty thousand surfing. And I bring in far less than that, running a bookstore that operates out of a bar on Venice beach. For California standards, it's practically poverty, but we don't need much. For Paul and I, we never did. We're lucky to have this place, my stepfather blessing us with a rent payment low enough to both piss our neighbors off and ensure that we still can cover food and utilities.

Paul and I met two years ago, at the Santa Monica pier, when we were side by side in the singles line for the rollercoaster. We had all of six minutes in line, the shuffle moving quickly, singles getting split up among the empty seats in a bored and orderly fashion.

He flashed a smile at me, and that was really all it took. Broad shoulders, tan skin that peeled a bit on his nose, blue eyes that looked like a fucking turquoise magic marker. He was in board shorts, a t-shirt, and flip flops with muscular, track-free arms and no hint of tattoos. It was like God plucked an Abercrombie & Fitch model from the sky and injected him with testosterone and sexuality. I smiled back.

We spent those six minutes talking, our words spilling out between laughs and chemistry. I instantly liked him, had one of those at-peace realizations that 'this is a good guy.' The type so good that women run over him, the type so good that he is often stuck in the friend-zone. But this guy? With his gorgeous looks and the I-will-fuck-you-in-this-line-right-now vibe? No woman was stupid enough to best friend this man. I wanted him, right there in that line, my panties sticking to me in the best way possible beneath my short cotton skirt.

We reached the front, our moment of separation, but were seated together, two of us in one bench, a ridiculous, never-should-happen moment, and I took the minute before liftoff to reach over, tugging the back of his head, his wide smile and soft lips telling me I wasn't crazy, that he wanted this every bit as much as I did. And I knew, in that kiss, in that brief moment of hotness, in which our mouths instantly knew every part of the other's soul, that I would fuck him. The minute—no, the second—the ride finished. I needed him inside me, needed his hands to grip my waist, his shirt to move off that beautiful chest and my bare breasts to replace it. I needed every inch of him against and inside of me. Then the bar jerked down, and we separated with a laugh.

"Ready?" he asked.

"Just prepare for screams." I grinned.

I was, and still am, a dramatic rider. I believe there's no point in doing something if you aren't going to do it with all of your heart. I raised my arms, I screamed bloody murder, and he loved every minute of it. We swept through the loading bay after one cycle, the operator amping the riders before pushing the button and letting us ride again.

The vibration of the seat underneath me, the closeness of pure sex beside me, the anticipation of what was to come ... I attacked him the moment the ride ended, grabbing his hand and tugging him out, the pounding between my legs reaching a fever pitch. I ran, pulling him along with me, our bodies weaving around families, couples, giant stuffed snakes, and dollar games of chance.

We broke from the crowd and moved faster, our flip-flops slapping against the wood boardwalk, the tinny laugh of children vaguely registering in my head. I broke right when I saw the opening and jogged down sandy steps, glancing behind me to make sure he was there. He was, his eyes bright and curious, his steps right behind mine, keeping easy pace with my frantic steps. "What are we ... where are we going?"

he called out. I ditched my sandals when I hit the sea of white and ran through hot sand, gripping his hand and pulling him along, under the boardwalk, past a few homeless tents and down toward the water, where the posts are thicker, the cover more enclosed, privacy at a barely-there standard. I waded into calf-high water, pulling and then pushing him against a square post, my hands frantic on his shirt, my mouth fighting the movement of clothes for another chance at that gorgeous mouth.

His hands pushed my thin tee up, over the curves of my bikini top, his firm fingers sliding the triangles of my bikini over, my breasts spilling free, his hands cupping and squeezing, his breath catching in my mouth. He pulled away, looking down, staring at my breasts in his hands, his head leaning down, his hands lifting me into the heat of his mouth. His mouth was incredible, soft yet firm, pliable against my delicate skin, his fingers' brush against my nipples soft and sweet. I could feel him, hard against my thigh, and I reached back, digging into my pocket for what I always kept there—just in case. Just in case I met a man who I couldn't resist.

He started at the touch of my fingers, dipping under the nylon of his shorts, his mouth coming off my breasts and looking at me, surprised. "Here?" This close, I could see tints of green in his blue eyes, the color of ocean water, glittering brilliantly against the brown sand of his skin.

"Yes, here. I need you." I met his eyes confidently as I said the words, my hands already sealing the deal, pulling him out— *oh my god, hard*—and sliding protection over him with one smooth motion. His eyes darkened, intensity stealing over them, and he turned us, trading places, pushing my back against the hard, wet span of wood, his hands lowering, gripping the back of my legs and sliding up, pushing my skirt higher, his hands gripping the my ass and lifting.

Then I was in the air, his pelvis underneath me, supporting me against the post, and his fingers were skimming the line of my bikini bottoms, traveling up the curve of my hip until he reached the tie, yanking quickly, his hand moving back down once the material of my suit was gone. His mouth left mine, a gasp in his tone as his fingers pushed inside, one digit and then two. "Jesus. Are you sure?"

A stupid question as I hung before him, my breasts exposed, legs wrapped around his waist, my need dripping a path for his cock. "Give it to me," I breathed. "Hard."

He didn't ask again, didn't do anything but prop me hard against the post, used his fingers to position himself at my entrance, and then he fucked. Quick strokes, his breath hard against my neck, his hands digging into the flesh of my ass, pulling and gripping the skin as he made his mark on my body. His fucks were wild, out of control, and I moaned against his neck, loving the fervor of his movements.

When I came, I cried out, his mouth quickly moving to mine, muffling the sound, as my body shook around his, my legs squeezing as intensity shook my body. It was too much, too great, the heat of my orgasm and clench of my sex, and I felt him as he came, the twitch and raw emotion that flowed through him, his breath gasping as he grunted, slowing his fucks and giving me a few final pushes.

"Oh my God," he whispered against my neck, his cock softening inside of me. "Oh my God. I think I'm in love with you."

He wasn't in love. Not yet. He was just surprised that a girl with perfect teeth, and a bred-in-the-Valley smile, would fuck a stranger under the Santa Monica pier. And I thought, as I dropped to my knees in the water and peeled off the condom, taking him into my mouth and sucking cum off his cock, that I would never see him again. That it would be that one fuckable moment and nothing else. But here we are, two years later and incredibly in love.

That's right. In *love*. Yes, I am still the hoochie who just got my brains fucked out on the weight bench. The one who has dated Stewart Brand, one of the most eligible bachelors in downtown Hollywood for the last two years. I know what you're thinking. That dropped jaw and disgusted look on your face? I've seen it before. But wait. Please. Don't judge me quite yet.

I am barefoot on the couch when Paul gets home, the door slamming open and shaking the framed ribbon that was his first ever surfing prize. I slide the headphones off my head, rising to my feet. "Hey lover," I say, wrapping my arms around his neck.

"Hey beautiful. How was life with the other half?"

"Bearable." I pull him tightly to me for a kiss. "I need you."

He welcomes me home with a kitchen fuck, my ass bare on the counter, legs wrapped tight around his waist. His mouth plays with my neck as he fucks, his pace smooth and unhurried, as if we have all of the time in the world. And, in a way, we do. Nothing to do today, no appointments or places to be. He whispers dirty things as his hands slide around and beneath me, gripping my ass and pulling me into his strokes. I come once, my legs tightening around him, my walls constricting and squeezing, his speed increasing enough to take me over the edge and gently back down. Then we move, his arms carrying me to the bed, his cock still hard and firm inside of me, and he lays me down. There, on our worn sheets, he rolls me onto my side, and takes me to orgasm another two times, finishing with a groan.

We lay entwined in each other's arms, the open window providing a strong breeze of salt and sand, washing over our damp skin. He pulls me closer, pressing a soft kiss on my neck. "I love you, Madd."

"I love you, too." And I do. I love this man, who has not one stressed out bone in his body. He concerns himself with two things: surfing and keeping me happy. I love his outlook on life, a Bob Marley style philosophy. We fuck, we surf, and we love. There isn't too much else to our life. To this half of my life.

"Waves are supposed to be strong this afternoon. Wanna ride some today?"

"I think I'll hit the bookstore. Log in a few hours. You go out this morning?"

"Yeah. Got up about five. Mavericks Invitational is in three weeks so I'll hit it hard 'til then."

Paul doesn't need to practice. He is a god on a stick. His arms and legs work in perfect synchronization, his body gliding and bending at the perfect moment to stay balanced. Watching him surf makes my heart pound and my body clench. It is pure sex, the push and pull of muscles in a graceful movement that displays his athleticism. He's consistently ranked in the top twenty surfers in the world, a ranking that means little when it comes to his finances. Every competition is a negative investment, unless he wins. If he wins, sponsors are happy and prize money covers a few months of rent. If he loses, he is out his travel expenses, and we eat Ramen until the next big event.

I close my eyes, twisting until my head is on his stomach, his hand automatically reaching for and running through my hair, pulling bits of blond and curling them around his fingers. I close my eyes, the movement soothing and familiar. Outside, some music starts up, the strands of reggae floating through the air and over our space. To Ziggy Marley's voice and against Paul's sun-kissed abs, I close my eyes and fall asleep.

I hate society's notion that there is something wrong with sex. Something wrong with a woman who loves sex. I've loved sex for as long as I can remember. I lost my virginity at fourteen, when Gus Blankenship showed me his penis behind the gym, and I got so hot and bothered that I let him put it in me. Right there, with hard gravel digging into my back, his excited acne-covered face above. It was the best forty-two seconds of my life thus far.

That was back in the day. When fourteen year olds were still pure, and not the makeup covered, push-up bra tramps they are today. Sixth grade sleepovers are now orgies where the girls fight over who's gonna get to suck the barely-handsome dad off first.

It's all wrong, the evolution of our innocent youth into cock-gobbling sluts. Which seems hypocritical coming from me, but it's not. I fuck because I love it, because I want to—it brings me pleasure. They fuck because they think that they have to—for the guy, for the queen-bee girl, for the proverbial 'fuck you' to society that they think it creates.

They have it so backwards, so twistedly screwed. Sex should be about mutual enjoyment, connection, the borrowing from another's fire at a moment when you want it most.

I pity them, with their glossy red lips and pierced belly buttons. Because, when it all comes to pass? When they 'grow up' and getting fucked during halftime is no longer cool but suddenly slutty? They will feel dirty. Used. Ruined. Because they did it for the wrong reasons.

My phone rings, shrill and demanding. I sigh, the ringtone reserved for only one individual.

"Would you like me to get that?" The soft voice of the masseuse matches the dim room, soothing sounds, and eucalyptus scent.

"Do you mind bringing it to me? I'll put it on silent." I push up, taking the cell and silencing the call, flipping the button on the side to mute any future interruptions. "Sorry about that." I lay back down, holding out the phone, the woman taking it from me with a gracious smile.

Mother. I will need to call her back, as soon as Kindi finishes melting every muscle off my body. Paul needs this, to let this woman work her magic on his sore back and tight legs. But that will never happen. Kindi is a Stewart perk, her oiled hands rubbing me down in the second floor of Stewart's skyscraper. That'd be combining my worlds, and as stupid as I am to have the two worlds, even I realize the danger in mixing their components. Overlapping cannot happen.

I take a deep breath and exhale, intentionally relaxing my shoulders, her fingers digging and pushing, breaking up a bundle of nerves, the pain excruciatingly pleasurable. I push all thoughts of Paul out of my head and focus on her hands.

HOLLYWOOD, CA

I grew up a charmed child of La Jolla. Nannies wiped my dirty ass, Christmas was spent in Aspen, and school uniforms shared closet space with miniature lines of Dior and Versace. I lived a privileged life between surfer chick and spoiled brat, sandy cheeks and wet bikinis chafing the leather seats of my ice blue BMW convertible. I smoked weed with friends in million-dollar mansions with ocean views while our parents cruised the Black Sea. I fucked preppy boys who wore Lacoste and Rolexes and played lacrosse. I was in a bubble of ridiculousness and grew up thinking that life never said no, credit cards were never declined, and happiness was a given.

Then my father, a hedge fund manager with a minor addiction to cocaine, drove off the manicured edge of a Malibu cliff, to the polished astonishment of a restaurant full of Orange County's upper society. The fact that his mistress, a surgically enhanced blonde three years older than me, was in the front seat, was hid from no one, and embraced by many of my mom's arch enemies. They died, drowned or killed by the cliffs. I didn't ask for particulars, and none were offered up.

Perfection, in that moment, became flawed and fragile. I never took anything for granted again.

Our money lasted another ten months, 'til the fat mortgage, civil lawsuits, and attorneys took it all. I spent my senior year at the public high school, my BMW repossessed, my school uniforms left in the closet of a home that the bank quickly seized. I was unceremoniously dumped into normality, courtesy of a mother fighting her own depression. If I had still had a cell phone at that moment in time, I could assure you that my lifelong 'friends' would not have answered my call.

Looking back, I see the turning point that occurred during that time. I miss my father, despite his shortcomings and mistakes. I loved him; I have pieces of him throughout my personality. But the person that I was becoming? The type of individual bred by easy wealth and never-told-no parenting? I was a bitch. A self-assured, my-way-or-the-highway bitch. I didn't appreciate what I had and demanded more at every turn. I am grateful that I got kicked in the ass. That I had a taste of reality before I traveled too far and that persona became permanent.

That happened to my mother. She was raised in those twenty thousand square foot mansions; she was given everything she ever wanted, right up until the moment that it all disappeared. She drowned herself in top-shelf martinis we couldn't afford, refusing to cook, clean, or pay bills—her breeding too far above such blue-collar work. I became the adult, she became the child, and we sank further until I moved out and she found a man. Now she is the wife and full-time dependent of Maurice Fulton, an old man who she can't possibly love, one who keeps her groomed and outfitted in his big house and keeps her glass filled. I speak to her occasionally, when I get the sadistic urge to see what a society-bred alcoholic sounds like.

Family is one thing I have in common with my men. We are all loners, floating through life unattached, except to each other. We don't talk about our pasts, our lack of familial ties. There is no point in dwelling on the darkness. Not when our new life is full of such light.

Five months before Paul, I met Stewart on the street in downtown Hollywood. It was November and snowing. Not thick, heavy snow that allowed snowmen and powder fights, but a light flurry that swirled through the air and fell softly on open tongues, melting upon contact. It doesn't snow in our part of the world—not normally, the barely-there flurries an event worth celebrating.

I was downtown, having met my stepfather's attorney to sign some paperwork. Halfway through our meeting, I noticed the snow, my feet bringing me to the window, hands and nose pressed to the glass like a child. I was anxious to move outside, to feel the soft flurries and to lift my face to the sky. When the meeting concluded, I ran down six flights of stairwell steps and burst into the frigid air.

I was spinning when I stumbled out of place and into the hard polish of his suit. His steps were moving, pausing only to right my stride before moving on. But my ankle turned in the stumble, and I let out a small cry of pain that had his eyes meeting mine, concern thick in the blue glint of his irises. He stopped, gripping my arms, his stare intent on my face. "Are you all right?"

I winced, pushing against his chest and put some weight on my ankle, moving away from him and gripping the metal rod of a street sign. "I'm fine." I glanced up, watching the erratic swirl of flakes, my mouth curving back into a smile. "It's snowing."

He dismissed the miracle of snow with one shrug of his suit. "Is your car close by?"

"It's just a few blocks up." I leaned against the pole, putting weight on my good foot. I held out my hand and watched as dots of white sprinkled its surface. I glanced over at him, my eyes distracted from the snow as I took in the gorgeous exterior that was this stranger. Custom suit stretched across a strong, tall build. Black hair, swept back and dotted with snow. Blue eyes staring at me with a mixture of impatience and concern. I smiled. "I'm good, really."

He sighed, glancing around, then stepped closer, holding out his arm. "May I ... please? Let me carry you inside. I can have a driver take you home."

I laughed. "And not be able to get back to my car? That is thoughtful, but driving won't be a problem, it's my other foot."

He stepped closer, his open hand brushing my side, and I started at the contact, the brush of touch electric. "Then I'll carry you to your car. Please." His eyes softened, the urgency in them gone, and I relaxed.

"If you insist." I smiled, giggling when he scooped me up, cradling me to his chest, his intense eyes staring bemusedly down at me.

"This is funny?" he questioned, a flow of minty fresh air floating down on me.

"Quite romantic, actually." His hands supported me easily, my weight not slipping and sliding through his arms. I leaned in, resting my head against the wool of his suit, the bump of our movement slightly rocky. "Take a right here. It might be a hair more than a few blocks." I discreetly inhaled, a delicious blend of vanilla and forest hitting my nose, and I burrowed my face further into his chest.

"What's your name?" The words vibrated through his chest, and I lifted my head, staring at the strong muscles of his neck, and had the insane urge to lift my mouth to them, to trail playfully kisses up, 'til I reached the fine shadow of his jaw, over that strong feature and to those lips. I swallowed.

"Madison. Decater."

He stopped walking, the abrupt change causing instability, my arms gripping his shoulders for balance, then snaking around his neck. He looked down into my face, smiling, the bright flash of white teeth against the stubble of his five-o-clock shadow breathtaking. "Stewart Brand. It's a pleasure to meet you."

"Same here."

He then asked me where I lived and what I did. We laughed over his lack of book knowledge and over his admission of no social life. We flirted, his hands tightened, and we walked two blocks past my car before I realized it and made him turn around.

We parted awkwardly, neither one of us wanting to step away, then his cell rang, and he glanced at his watch, muttering a curse. He passed me a business card while stepping away, answering the phone and bringing it to his ear. "Call me," he mouthed. "Please." Then with a wink, he left, talking quickly, his steps turning into a jog as he headed back up the street. I hobbled into the car and watched his back disappear, waiting to see if he would glance back. But he didn't, and I stuffed his card into my purse and left, my tender ankle almost causing my Suzuki to sideswipe an adjacent Mercedes.

I sat on the card for a week, occasionally pulling it out and running my fingers over the surface. Women shouldn't call men. We should be pursued, should play the offhand, casual game until the men tackled us to the ground with flowers and affection. But his hurried exit, the urgency on his face when the phone rang, didn't give us the customary time to find pen and paper, to exchange numbers. I bent the card slightly in my hand, considered tossing it the trash and ending this dilemma once and for all.

But I didn't. Day nine, I called, an efficient female taking down my information in a manner that guaranteed no call back. Day ten, she called back, five times friendlier and set a lunch appointment for Stewart and I three weeks later. I repeated the date uncertainly, expecting for her to be mistaken, and her cheerful tone hardened slightly as she informed me that he was a very busy individual, and she had shifted an entire day to accommodate that time frame. I took the date. Twenty-eight months later, I don't need her to shift schedules. I get my stolen time in the wee hours of the night, or during a business dinner, or if an appointment cancels and I am in the area to grab a quick bite or a fuck on his desk.

Snow. Falling snow is what brought us together. That and his hurried life, which collided us in the first place.

HARPOONING: [VERB]
COPPING WOOD WHILE SURFING.

I am woken in the night, a hand on my shoulder, shaking me gently. "Maddy. " Soft lips brush my neck, the rough scruff of unshaven skin tickling my cheek.

I roll, pulling up on the sheet, the cool night air cold on my bare chest. "Stop," I mumble.

"Come on," Paul whispers, sliding under the sheet, the warm heat of his skin settling over mine, his weight gently held by knees and arms. His kisses drift over my body, the hot nip of his lips traveling up my stomach, over my breasts, before settling on my lips.

"I'm sleeping," I whisper between long kisses, his body settling deeper, pinning me to the bed, my legs spreading and wrapping around him.

"No you're not." He grins at me, pulling the blanket over both of our heads, his face close in the darkness.

"Yes," I reply firmly. "I am." I reach between our bodies, adjusting his cock so it lies against his stomach, in a position to better stimulate me when it hardens. He grinds slightly against me, my hand gripping him firmly, feeling the reaction in his cock, the thickening of skin underneath my fingers.

"I like you when you sleep." He leans down, taking a long taste of my mouth and slowly thrusts his pelvis, my hand releasing him, the firm friction right *there* against my clit as it should be. "Waves are at six feet," he says against my mouth, a flash of teeth shining in the darkness.

"So ride them."

"I'd rather ride something else right now."

"Me too."

I don't need to move his cock. His hips take care of that, a small downward shift and his hardness making the transition easy, my wet entrance more than ready for fulfillment. Then he resumes his strokes, slow and perfectly, inside me, the air under the blanket hot with passion. And when I yank the blanket off his head, the cool air is needed, as we both arch our bodies into the darkness of oblivion.

I dress, slipping on bikini bottoms and a surf shirt, linking my hand through his and jogging down the garage steps. We grab our boards and move, quiet through dark streets, nodding to familiar faces, the homeless and beggars who never sleep, discomfort or addiction keeping them awake. When our feet hit the sand we run, eager to fly, the shock of cold water taking me the final step into wide awake. We paddle until my arms ache, we ride until the waves calm, and then we lay back on salty boards and watch the sun rise, reflecting sparks of fire across the tops of ripples.

You don't understand the true awesomeness of nature until you watch the sun rise on water that stretches across half the world. Or until you lay back on the board in the pitch black of night and listen to the world sleep. Until you feel the tug of water and know that you are dancing with a partner that could dip you into death should it feel the need. It is intoxicating, the heartbeat of the ocean. It flows through my blood; it sucks at my heart and pumps breath through my lungs.

I hear Paul's call and turn, realizing that he has paddled halfway in and is waiting. The crowds will soon come, the hordes of tourists who have traveled across the country to play in our backyard. Now is the time to return, and let the strangers borrow a piece of our life. I roll to my stomach, and paddle after Paul, the rising sun prickling warm on my bare legs.

SPEEDBUMP: [NOUN]
SOMEONE WHO STANDS IN
THE WAY OF A GOOD RIDE.

DANA

Some might call my behavior stalking. My opinion is if you love the person, it gives you some justifiable leeway. My behavior this evening ... leeway doesn't really excuse it. It's borderline creepy. I sicced my assistant on Stewart. Told her I'd give her two hundred dollars for each event where she could reasonably predict his presence. It took her three weeks, but she found one. His business partner's birthday party at Livello on Friday night. She called the restaurant, verified that the reservations were at nine o'clock that evening, and we discussed the chances of him being present. A hundred percent chance of him being invited, and we were thinking a twenty-five percent chance of attendance. I was grasping that narrow percentage with the tenacity of a drowning woman.

It's ten, and I am huddled in the back corner of the lobby, nursing a bottled water, an Elle magazine held open before me. My mission is simple. If he is alone, approach him. And if he is with someone, scope her out. I'm giving myself 'til eleven, then I'm going to bail. Toss Belinda her two hundred bucks and go soak my feet in Epsom salts. I curse the three-inch heels I put on this morning. Next stakeout, I'll wear flats.

The door opens, and in a burst of cool air and perfume, they enter.

God, three years hasn't changed him. He is smiling, and that is the first thing I notice. Holding the door open for her, his hand moves to cup her waist when she moves through the door in front of him. Their cheeks are flushed, her giggle reaching back into the dark corner where I sit, a curl of jealousy snaking through me at the sound. I sink in my seat, watching them closely, noticing everything, the brush of his hand against her ass, the look in his eyes when she grabs the fabric of his shirt and presses into his chest, his head dipping down for a kiss. They are quickly escorted into the restaurant, away from my eyes, and I strain for a final glimpse of him, but only see the back of the maitre'd.

I exhale, setting down the magazine and lean back in my seat, lifting my purse off the ground and setting in on my lap with a heavy sigh. There is no point in staying to see them leave. I saw everything I needed in that brief moment. The look in his eyes ... she is not a fling. Not an escort who he hires for events. That was the look of love.

My hands tighten around my purse.

MADISON

It didn't take long for Stewart and I to fuck. The sweet circumstance of our meeting quickly turned to heat, chemistry sizzling across the linen tablecloths of our first date. For the second date, two weeks later, I told his icy secretary I'd meet him at his place, intent on putting the little time she had penciled in to good use. She extended the appointment, giving me a full two hours, which I took to be a good sign. Two weeks later, I handed my keys to a freckle-faced valet, signed in with the security desk at Stewart's condo, and was yanked inside the moment he opened the door.

He crab-walked me backward, my hands reaching for his face, pulling it to mine, our first kiss frantic. "Tell me if I'm reading this wrong." He rushed out, between kisses. "Is this too fast?"

I bit back a laugh, unbuttoning the front of my shirtdress and dropping the material to the floor, nothing but bare skin underneath. "You tell me, is it?" I stepped away, watched his eyes devour me, his expression turning dark, his hand running rough through his hair.

Then his mouth and his hands were on me, and we didn't have the breath to utter words for a full hour. We started there, against the wall, with kisses and touches, my own hands pulling at his clothes, 'til he was naked before me, and my breath caught at his build, his body a tight coil of muscles that all seemed to center and point on a package that would have made my first boyfriend duck his head in shame. He lifted me, my legs wrapping around his waist, and carried me to a bedroom.

I didn't notice the heated floors or the custom blinds or the six thousand dollar rug. I only noticed the heat of our bodies, the perfect fit, the exact blend of control and fury that took my body from above, from behind, and from below.

Forty-five minutes after setting foot in his condo, he straddled me. Breathing hard, his face tight in concentration, his hands running over the skin of my breasts, he leaned forward and kissing me, pushed away my hands when I reached for him. His cock bobbed between us, brushing my stomach, a plastic slap of latex against my skin. "Don't," he groaned. "I'm too close. Give me a moment."

But I wanted it, was high on orgasm and his fucks, and anxious to see the result of our work. I smiled at him, reaching down with a firm hand, and slid the condom off, his slick head exposed, my hand working up and down as I looked up into his face.

He squeezed his eyes tight, his breath coming out in short spurts. "Madison, I can't, you're—" He bucked his hips, groaning my name, my hand hard and fast on his shaft, watching in excitement as he came, multiple shots on my chest. His head dropped back as he finished, a long sigh releasing. He collapsed to the side, his limbs heavy on the bed, his eyes closed, a smile on his face.

I rolled, unmindful of the sheets, resting my head on his bicep, my body relaxed after an hour of orgasms and pounding.

Minutes passed, no sound other than our breaths and the whip of the fan, no need to speak, no need for compliments or unnecessary conversation.

Then he moved, rolling to his side, our faces close, his eyes studying mine. "How are you single?"

I looked into his eyes, at the bright blue sparks of his pupils. "I don't need a boyfriend."

"Women rarely need the things they want." He smiled, running a free hand gently along the inside of my arm.

"I'm not exactly normal," I offered. His mouth curved at the words, light entering them, a sarcastic response on the tip of his tongue. I waved his comeback off. "I don't mean that in a good way. You and I? Having sex so quickly? It wasn't because your penthouse or your gorgeous blue eyes blew me away. It was sex, great sex, but just for pleasure. What we just did … I'm not expecting anything from you because of it. I don't need to make 'this' anything more than what it is right now."

He frowned. "So you want to use me … you *are* using me. For sex."

I laughed. "Oh, please, it's every man's perfect scenario. Don't give me that guilt trip."

His frown twitched slightly at the corners. "And what if I want more?"

"I don't think you have time for more."

I knew, from the start, what I was signing up for. And I made sure he knew the same. That I was a sexual creature, who wouldn't stand by and wait to be beckoned. I lived my normal life, with bits of Stewart's cock sprinkled in when he had time. And that lasted for a bit, 'til he started getting attached and decided he didn't want me screwing strangers any more.

"I want you to find a boyfriend." Stewart said gruffly, while I was pinned against the wall of his office, his rigid cock inside of me. It was nine o'clock on a Tuesday night, everyone with any sanity gone, a uniformed cleaner already sticking his head in and catching us in the act.

"What?"

He thrust upward, making me moan, pulling my hips downward slightly, 'til the depth made me ache. "A boyfriend. Someone to fuck you when I am busy, someone who can take you on dates, and rub your feet, and listen to you talk about your day."

"I fuck when you're busy." The statement caused his eyes to darken, his thrusts to increase in force and speed.

He knew this. Knew I wasn't exclusively his. It was a choice he made, his addiction to success and files and stock prices too time-consuming to allow for more than a night or two a week of fucktime. And our time together was often like this—squeezed in at a time when stress lined his face, and meetings or emails were only a step or two away.

"I don't like you fucking a bunch of strangers. It's not safe. And you deserve more than that."

I wished he would stop talking, the words causing his movement to stop, his serious expression putting a damper on my arousal. "Let's talk about it later."

He continued on, ignoring my suggestion. "You deserve someone who will be there for you everyday. Who will rub your feet and take you to dinner, and take you to the doctor when you're sick."

"So you want me to ditch you for someone with more time?"

He growled, gripping my skin and lifting me, my arms wrapping around his neck for security, as he carried me across the room and deposited me on his desk. "Fuck no. I will never allow someone to take you from me." He ran his hands possessively down my front, pulling up my tank top and caressing the bare breasts beneath, his hands firm and strong, cupping my breasts like he owned them, dropping his face down and taking one in his mouth. "But I will lose you soon enough to someone who can shower you with time and affection. You need an everyday man to satisfy those needs." He glanced up as his pace resumed, that dark glitter of intensity that I loved returning to his eyes. "But I will always own your heart. And this man would be second to me in your heart."

I smiled, wrapping my legs around his hips and squeezing. "You can't control my heart, Stewart."

He lowered himself to me, bending over the desk as he fucked me—deep, possessive fucks that shot drugged pleasure through me with each stroke. Gripping my arms and pinning them to the desk, he took a long, deep taste of my mouth before breaking away and staring into my eyes. "I can sure as hell try."

I closed my eyes, gripping his hips, and let him fuck me through another two orgasms before he came, in my mouth, his eyes glued to mine as he pumped himself onto my tongue. I thought he would drop the 'boyfriend' talk—thought that it was mid-sex ridiculousness that would never be spoke of again. But he pressed the issue, revisiting the topic enough times that I realized his sincerity. He worried about me. My safety, my happiness. Worried about losing me due to lack of attention. He wanted me to have a steady fuck, wanted someone to make up for the slack he couldn't provide. He wanted someone safe, friendly. Someone I wouldn't leave him for, but that would make me happy. He wanted Paul; I just hadn't found him yet.

So I continued fucking strangers, my libido as aggressive as ever. And then, on that day in Santa Monica, I met Paul. I fucked Paul. And he was different. Paul was, as he stared into my eyes and fucked me in the surf, someone Stewart would approve of.

Safe.

Friendly.

Sweet.

Paul has changed since that day. He is more possessive of me than he once was. Not during our daily life, but often our sex is fired with competitiveness, his cock claiming me as if he has something to prove. He is not safe, and Stewart has every cause to be worried. They both own my heart now, an equal division fought over by two sets of blue eyes.

My phone rings and I glance at it. LOVER displays across its front. *Stewart.* I opened the phone. "Hey babe."

"Hey. You free Thursday night? I have a work thing ... need a date."

"Sure."

"Perfect. I'll connect you to Ashley." There is a click and a few tones before the cheerful voice of his assistant fills my ear. We chat for a few minutes, and then I hang up.

"Was that him?" Paul's strokes across the board continue, slow patient swipes of wax protection. We are in the garage, the door up, our cars pulled into the alley, bikers occasionally whizzing through the open space. I've already waxed my board, my job quickly and haphazardly done, no real desire present to do a thorough job. But Paul takes his time, stretching the task out, his eyes careful on his work, his strokes sure and familiar.

"Yeah. I've got a thing to attend tomorrow night. I'll be back in the morning. When do you leave for Costa Rica?" I watch his shoulders for tension, his jaw for rigidity, but he is calm, peace in his eyes, an easygoing manner in his movements.

"End of next week. I'll be gone four or five days, depending on the flight." He sets down the wax, walking around the board and leans back against my car, pulling me by the waist, into his arms.

"I'm gonna miss you, Madd."

I smile, leaning into his chest. "I'll be here when you get back."

"Promise?"

"Promise." I lift my chin, and he kisses me, his hands pulling me tight, his mouth needy on mine. This is Paul's worry. That one day he will return, and I will be gone. That I will choose Stewart and not him. He doesn't mind sharing, but losing me terrifies him.

I flip through book titles, pulling out spines and sliding in new ones, running the alphabet over my tongue, making sure that everything was in its proper place, J.D. Robb sitting after James Patterson and before Nora Roberts. I feel him before I see him, the creak of the floor behind me announcing a visitor's weight, the air carrying the scent of sunscreen and sweat.

I don't pause, my fingers pushing and pulling on titles, intent on filing these last three books before my mind gets sidetracked, and I have to start the whole damn alphabet again.

"You know ebooks are going to replace these pretty soon." The gentle, confident male drawl slows my movements, my mouth curving into a smile despite my best attempt to keep a cool exterior.

I squeeze the last book into place and stand, turning toward Paul. "Hey—words like that'll get you killed around here."

He scoffs, crossing his arms across a broad chest, covered in a tank and a golden tan. "You don't have a dangerous bone in your body."

I walk around the half bookcase between us, 'til I stand in front of him. "You're right about that. I'm in sore need of a dangerous bone inside of me."

He groans, his eyes turning from playful to feral in a moment, his hand reaching around me and pulling me tight to him. His other hand joins in, both of them gripping and pulling my ass and pushing my pelvis up into his body, tight enough that the ridge of his erection digs into me. He lets out a loud, shuddering breath as he lowers his mouth to mine. "You want me to fix that situation?"

"Oh yeah." I grin, reaching up and tugging his head down, my tongue taking up the playful game, flicking into his open mouth, exploring the taste of him as his hands pull me tighter against his hard body.

"I want to fuck you right here," he whispers against my mouth.

"So do it." My hands slide under his shirt, traveling over the lines of abs, his mouth catching as I move my hands lower, under the hem of his board shorts, my fingers encountering the curly patch of hair there.

He chuckles, moving his mouth off mine and kissing the top of my head. "I'll take care of you later. I just wanted to stop in and say hi."

I look up at him. "Fine. I'm closing up shop at four. Want me to find you on the water then?"

He cradles my head in his hands, his eyes trailing over the lines of my face, as if he is memorizing the features. "I'll be there. Tonight is when you have that thing?"

I nod. "I'll be back in the morning."

He grins, my playful boy back. "Then I'll be sure to take care of you this afternoon."

I yank him forward, wanting to feel the brush of hardness before he leaves me alone. "You better."

He gives me a final kiss before releasing my face, tossing out a carefree smile before ducking through the entrance and disappearing into the bright California sun.

I understand that you hate me. That you curse me for my greed. But if I am okay with it, and they are okay with it, how is it anyone else's right to judge?

CAVEFISH: [NOUN]
PALE SURFER

DANA

I stub my cigarette out and watch the bar, listening idly as Shannon Marks blabs the explicit details of last night's blind date. I tune in occasionally, nodding politely and cracking a smile when the occasion seems to call for it. But mainly, I just watch the bar. *I saw her. Stewart's blonde princess.* I was sitting here, minding my own business, sipping fresh coffee and munching on biscotti when she trotted by. Flashing a smile to a pothead who sat on the curb, she entered the bar without a second glance around. That was forty-five minutes ago.

I light another cigarette.

Venice beach. Not the location I expected to find her in. From my first impression, at Livello, she had seemed too upscale for this area—her glowing skin and sparkly white teeth speaking of good breeding, the dress one that appeared to be four-figure fabulous. I almost didn't recognize her here, in cutoff shorts and a plaid, long-sleeved button-up, aviators perched on her head, long tanned legs ending in a pair of leather flip-flops. But it's hard to miss a girl like her. And I've thought about that night too much to be sane. Replayed it over and over again in my head. The glow on her face, the look in his eyes. Stewart, barely aged, one hundred percent the man I knew—save the grin on his face. The grin, the glint, of a man in love. That, sadly, was unfamiliar to me. I take a sip of coffee. Venice Beach. Yep, not what I expected. Then again, who am I to talk? I'm sitting here in a wool suit, sweating my ass off, all in hopes that I might run into Paul.

Paul. The other man in my heart, also MIA in my life. His absence pulls at my soul. Paul, the lost lamb of our family. What happened to Jennifer wasn't his fault. Things happen, regardless of all of our best intentions and precautions. Things happen, and when disaster struck, we lost him. He was always too sensitive, too caring, too loving. Quick to accept blame when it wasn't cast on him, quick to perceive if someone was mad or if feelings were hurt. He carried the happiness of our family on his shoulders, as if his young frame could support so much pressure. And that summer, ten years ago, was a bomb to that structure, a heavy cannonball dropped onto a little boy's house of sticks. We should have known he wouldn't recover. We should have known that it would push him away. Now, he lives as if that event never happened. As if Jennifer, and the rest of us, never existed.

I think the mere presence of us causes him pain. We are nothing but a walking billboard of what used to be. So he pretends we aren't here. And he walks through life with a smile on his face.

I don't know if that makes me happy or sad. I am relieved that he is happy; in press photos his grin stretches wide and easily, videos show that his step has a bounce in it. But I am sad for the brother I have lost. One who seems like he will never return home.

He lives around here somewhere. I don't have his number, can't find anything but a manager's number on the promotional website bearing Paul's pseudonym. The pseudonym irks me, a visible sign indicating his separation from our family. *Linx.* A stupid last name, picked by a nineteen year old kid with more pussy and dreams than he knew what to do with.

I exhale a burst of dirty air and glance towards the waves. The videos on his website show him here—attacking waves with the same ferocity he exhibited as a kid. So when Shannon wanted some gossip time, I suggested Venice Beach, hoping to kill two birds with one stone.

I take a sip of coffee and glance at my watch, my mind bouncing off Paul and back to the surprise sighting of Stewart's blonde. Fifty-two minutes. Who sits in a bar at two o'clock on a Monday afternoon for almost an hour? I push back from the chair; Shannon's dialogue pauses, my eyes glancing down to see her looking up with a look of surprise. "Where're you going?"

"Just a minute," I mutter, throwing my bag over my shoulder and zig-zagging through the crowd. Then I pull on the handle and step into the bar.

A woman should be dressed properly to go into battle. But I wasn't expecting to confront Stewart's Barbie this morning. I was only hoping to see Paul. So I wore an outfit Paul would recognize me in. I could envision the exact moment when he saw me. How his eyes would light up, and he would toss an arm over my shoulder, a soft kiss snuck in and placed on my cheek. And, in that moment, everything would be perfect. He would understand I still love him. That I will always love him—no matter what. And he will hug me and tell me that he loves me, too. That he will allow me to be a part of his life once again.

So I wore a suit, my normal skin for work and my non-existent social life. Paul would recognize a suit. It would stand out on the boardwalk. Cause him to stare a little longer, long enough to see my face and know. But now, walking into the bar filled with flip-flops and tan bodies, I wish I had at least worn my good heels. Prada would help me have the confidence to approach this woman. Prada would hold my hand and whisper in my ear that I am cool enough, hip enough, to approach this woman who is probably ten years my junior.

My eyes take a moment to adjust to the dark, neon lights coming into focus, the floor beneath my heels sticky. Only two figures at the bar, neither of which are blonde. The bartender, a redheaded pixie who shoulda worn sunscreen earlier in life, raises her chin at me. "What'cha need?"

My palms are suddenly clammy, and I wipe them down the front of my skirt, trying to think of some plausible need for my presence. "Do you have a restroom?"

She pops her gum, the crude, loud crack grating my nerves. "It's outside, past the bookstore. Down that hall." She points, and my eyes follow the path to a dingy hall, just past an open doorway. Glossy paperbacks are stacked on either side of the door, on wooden chairs that seem to sag beneath their weight. Curiosity makes my eyes linger, the reggae music from inside draws me closer to the door.

An arm chooses to snake out the door, startling me, coming from the height of a small child, pushing a heavy hardback out the door until it bumps into an adjoining stack. I step forward, peering inside, and see Stewart's blonde sitting cross-legged on the floor, books stacked all around her. *She works here.* The realization that she is not a barfly is relieving. I step backward, but her head snaps up, and our eyes meet for one terrifying moment.

She smiles. "Please don't leave. I can turn the music off if it bothers you."

"Oh no, it doesn't bother me." I wipe my annoyingly sweaty hands on my skirt, trying to find my mindset. Why had I come in here? What was my ball-busting plan of attack? Suddenly, my lack of designer shoes seems to be the least of my poor planning. "I was just looking for the bathroom."

She frowns regretfully, a ridiculously adorable gesture that makes me want to throttle her. "Damn. I was hoping for a reader. It's been crickets today." She stands, brushing off her shorts, leaving the pile of books behind. "Want me to show you the way?"

"No, it's okay." I glance around. It's a small space, a few rows squeezed into a small room lined with floor-to-ceiling shelves, shiny new books squeezed next to worn paperbacks with broken spines.

"I know that look. What's your weakness? Steamy billionaires with foot-long junk? Or a serial killer taking out half the women in Mississippi?" She shoots me a wicked grin, winking conspiratorially.

I blush, hating the smile that is fighting its way to my face. This is not how this is supposed to go. She shouldn't be cute or likable. I had expected upper crust, snooty, digging perfectly manicured fingers as far into Stewart's money pile as they could possibly go. "Janet Evanovich."

"Oooh! I knew I liked you." She jogs past me, humming along with the music as she drags a stool over to a shelf and stands, reaching up and trotting her fingers over titles. "You want the latest?"

"Sure."

"Have you read Stephanie Bond?"

I glance around the store, trying to pick up clues in the brief moment of her distraction. "Uhh … no."

She jumps off the stool, crouching down briefly and skimming over a second shelf, quickly snatching a book from the rack and tilting her head toward the register. "Anything else before I ring you up?"

I shake my head, reaching into my pocket for some cash.

"If you like Evanovich, you gotta check out Bond, too." She held up the second book. "It's used, so I'm gonna toss it in no charge. Just ignore the worn pages. She is freakin' awesome. If you get a chance." She shrugs. "Check it out."

I smile, counting out bills and passing them over. "Thank you—I will."

She bags the books and walks around the counter, handing me the green plastic bag with a smile. "Thanks for coming in. You want me to show you to the bathroom?"

Right. My imaginary need to pee. I shake my head. "I'm good. Thanks for the book."

I take a right out of the store, walking down the dim hall and locking myself in the dirty bathroom; I stand in the middle of the germ-infested space, trying not to touch anything. I take a deep breath and try to relax. Two minutes later, I use a paper towel to flush the toilet and open the door handle. I avoid looking into the bookstore, walking quickly through the dark bar and back into the bright light. The bench where I sat with Shannon is empty, a pink post-it stuck to her spot, an intense frowny face drawn on it in blue ballpoint pen. I glance around, seeing no sign of her, and crumple the sticky note, dumping my coffee into the trash, before casting one, final look for Paul. Then me, and my green bag of deception, leave the sandy boardwalk of Venice Beach.

MADISON

I am, for the next two years and three months, sterile. Then it will be time to pull out the hormone implant in my arm and replace it with a fresh one, and I can make that humongous decision again. To have a kid or not have a kid. That is the question. It was an easy decision two years ago. But I am already waffling now. In two years, I will probably be beside myself with the hefty choice. In a way, choosing a kid will be like choosing between my boys. It will be a conversation I will have to have with both of them, and I can already foresee their stance on it. Stewart won't have time for a child and will tell me so without hesitation. Any financial obligation he would support. But anything more … I'd be on my own. It's just the facts of his life. Paul will ask what makes me happy. And whatever I say, he will go with. It is how our relationship has always been. He does what makes me happy. It is why he accepts the fucked up threesome that we currently live. While Stewart wants me to have a second man to keep me off the streets, to keep me from being lonely, to keep me in his life—Paul accepts that I have a second man because it was what he signed up for. And now, as in the beginning, he'd rather have half of me than none of me.

Paul's and my first experience, under the Santa Monica Pier, led to dinner—meat lovers pizza under the dim lights of Joe's, cold beers downed, our bare legs brushing under the slanted brick bar top, knowing smiles exchanging space with flirtatious looks.

I thought that'd be it, but he persisted, got my number, called the next day. Showed up at the bookstore and pestered me 'til he snagged a second date. He didn't have to work too hard. I knew who he was, had wandered down to the surf after Bip went oh-my-God-that's-Paul-Linx crazy, spilling words like 'surfing god' and 'sweetheart' as if he was *onceinalifetime* special. I sat on the beach, sand smudging up my dress and sticking to my skin, and watched him on his board, watched the speed and dare of his ride, and let my mind wander down the what-if road. What if I went on a second, then third, then fourth date? What about Stewart? What about his idea of a second, consistent boyfriend? Could I bring up that scenario? And if I did, how would Paul respond?

I watched him, admired the flex of muscles as he crouched, then jumped into the water, emerging with a big smile, his gaze catching and lingering on me in the sand, a question of recognition in his eyes. Then he waved, the smile broadening, and I waved, and I knew I would have to try.

I broached the subject on our fourth date, at which point I had grown a little attached to his quick smile and always-ready cock. I waited 'til after sex, when we were stretched out on his bed, his hand running gently down the line of my back, the room quiet, save our contented breaths.

"Bring many girls here?" I teased, the words playful, the thoughtful look he gave me not.

He reached over, dragging me atop him 'til my head rested on his chest, my bare breasts on his stomach. "Not since I met you."

"Well, that's an impressive feat," I joked. "Seeing as we've screwed in this bed ... What? Three of the last four days?" I pushed up with my arms, crawling forward with my legs and straddled him. I tucked my hair behind my ear. "No girlfriend's clothes hanging in that closet?" I tilted my head to the door—an accordion-style set that was probably, ten years earlier, painted white.

He stretched back his arms, locking them behind his head and studied me, his face serious. "Why would you be here if I had a girlfriend?"

I shrugged. "Maybe she's busy. Out of town." His eyes follow me, staying on my face. "Maybe she doesn't care."

"I wouldn't be with someone if they didn't care," he said softly.

My eyes, which had been tracing the lines of his chest, his shoulders, the muscles enhanced by his position, finally came to his eyes, blue I had been avoiding as I attempted to find words that were unspeakable. "I ... have someone ..." His abs tensed underneath me, and his hands loosened beneath his head, his face tightening as he listened. "Someone I date—it's not an exclusive thing." I rush out the words, watching his features relax a bit. "He doesn't care. I mean, he cares, but he doesn't mind me dating other people. He's too busy for a full-time relationship."

"And?"

My eyes pulled back to his, surprised at the resolve behind him, the insistence to wait out this conversation until it reached final destination. I grimaced and pulled the band-aid off with one, painful rip, anxious to get it off and move the hell on.

"This guy ... he's a part of my life. I love him. I just wanted to put it out there. I don't know what you're looking for, if it's a fuck buddy or—"

"I want a relationship," he interrupted me, his face unreadable, and I fidgeted slightly on his hips.

It was too early to ask him the question, but I was already there, and he was waiting. Waiting while I was treading water, trying to figure out whether to dive deeper or swim for shore. Wondering if Stewart was worth this headache, while knowing, before my mouth even opened, that he was. "With me? I know it's early to ask that, but—"

"Yes. I want a relationship with you." His voice was quiet but firm, his hands sliding up my legs and stopping on my thighs. He looked at me as if he was completely in control of his emotions, utterly sure of the words coming out of his mouth. I yearned for that resolution, for that decision-making ability that he seemed to so cavalierly hold.

"I'm not available," I whispered. "Not fully. I do want a relationship with you. And it'd be exclusive ... except for him.

If we dated, he would still be in my life. That's something you'd have to be okay with."

His face darkened, his hands tightening slightly on my skin. "You'd date both of us?"

I nodded silently, unable to look away from the train wreck that was occurring between our eyes. "I love him," I said simply. I did. I had fallen for Stewart quickly, despite the gaps of time that kept us apart, despite the little that I saw him. He just … stayed with me. And it felt like every man I was with, every other touch I felt, was just a hollow substitute 'til I could have him again. Until Paul. Paul's touch, Paul's smile. It tugged at me in a new way. And I hoped, desperately, as I straddled him in that rundown duplex, a siren sounding one street over, that he would understand. That he would agree.

He didn't agree. I could see the fight on his face, the inner turmoil that pulled him this way or that. He sighed, sitting up, our position changing, and wrapped his arms around my waist, pulling me tightly to him, crushing my breasts against the muscle of his chest, his lips putting one soft kiss on my neck. "I can't," he whispered. "I'm sorry, Madd."

It was the first time he called me that. I liked hearing it on his lips, even if it was attached to such a horrid decision. I left his place fifteen minutes later, wanting, hoping, he would say the nickname again. Hoping I would hear it roll off his tongue one last time. But he didn't. He only hugged me close, kissed the top of my head, and studied my eyes, as if he could find out some secret answer that lay in their depths.

The second time I heard the nickname was one week later when he showed up at the bookstore, his face flushed, his eyes intense, and told me that he changed his mind.

"I don't like it," he muttered, running a hand through his hair, biting his bottom lip with a look of raw need that had me gripping the paperback in my hand a little tighter. "But ... I haven't been able to stop thinking about you. If it's what you want ... what you need. I'll give it a try."

We celebrated our new union right then, right there, pushing books aside and closing the doors, and he lowered me to the floor, his mouth frantic on me, ownership in every touch of his hands.

I think he was surprised at how easy it turned out to be. The seamless union our lives took. The separation played a big part in that. The separation of my two worlds. That was, and still is, the key that keeps this whole production running.

Now, two years later, I lie on his back, its firm strength golden in the morning light. He paddles, his muscles working smoothly underneath me, stroke after stroke that carries us farther and farther from shore, the sounds of the shore disappearing, replaced with sea gulls and ocean surf. He takes us out, 'til the waves subside and there is only calm, smooth rocking every ten seconds, my eyes closed, head flat against his back. Silence. No need to say anything, do anything that will break this perfect moment.

"I love you." His words quiet.

I know. My unspoken thought floats away from our bodies. "I love you, too."

My men are so different, yet similar in so many ways.

Their eyes. A similar tint of blue, but Paul's smile at me with carefree abandonment and Stewart's pierce my heart with their dark intensity.

Their bodies. Paul's naturally muscular, his arms developed from hours of surfboard paddling, his abs ripped from balancing on a board, his thighs and calves strong from jumping, balancing, and kicking through currents. Stewart's body, attacked like everything else in his life, with fierce devotion, aggression worked out with miles on a treadmill, weight lifting, sit-ups, pull-ups, and calisthenics.

Their love. Paul loves me with unconditional warmth, his affection public and obvious, his arms pulling me into him, his mouth littering my body with frequent kisses. Stewart loves me with a tiger's intensity, his need taking my breath away, his confidence in our relationship strong enough to not be bothered by the presence of another man. He stares into my soul as if he owns it, and shows his love with money, sex, and rare moments of time.

Tonight is one of those rare moments. I have his attention, his cell phone is away, and he is staring at me as if I contain everything needed to make his world whole. I step forward, toward his seated form, the dress hugging my form to perfection. He sits up in the chair, spreading his knees and patting his thigh, indicating where he wants me. I sit sideways on his thigh, my eyes held by his, his hand stealing up and running lightly along my bare back. "You are breathtaking." His voice gruff, he leans forward and places a light kiss on my neck. "And you smell incredible."

"Thank you. You clean up pretty well yourself." And he does. In a suit that no doubt costs more than my dress, he looks every bit the successful executive he is. Short, orderly hair. Clean-shaven chin. Those intense eyes staring out of a strong face. "Is the car here?"

"It's downstairs. But it can wait." He runs a hand up my knee, sliding the material of the cocktail dress up.

I wait, my breath becoming shallow, my concentration focused on the path of his fingers as they travel higher, taking their time, the tickle of rough skin against soft flesh. He leans over, brushing a quick kiss over my lips and then moves lower, soft kisses making the path down the line of my jaw, whispers against my neck, and deepening in touch when they reach my collarbone. His hand caresses my thigh, the brush of his thumb moving higher until it is just breaths from my sex. I groan, sliding my hips forward, but his hand stops me, gripping my thigh and holding me still. "Not yet. Let me enjoy you for a moment."

There is the sound of approaching footsteps, and I open my eyes to see a suited man, our driver, round the corner and stop short when we come into view. His eyes drop respectfully, and he speaks softly. "Mr. Brand, I'll be downstairs with the car when you are ready."

Stewart mutters something unintelligible, the man taking the cue and leaving, the firm pull of the door behind him leaving us alone. Stewart's hands push apart my legs, moving the fabric of my dress aside and leaving me bare and open to his eyes. He looks down, examining the exposed skin, his mouth curving into a smile. "No panties?" His eyes flick up to mine.

"They're in my purse. I figured they would be useless until we got to the event."

"That," he says softly, his fingers teasing the edge of my lips, circling the edge of my sex in slow, tantalizing brushes, each touch closer but not yet *there*, "is why I love you. You know me so well."

His eyes stare at me, dark pools of lust and want. While Paul and I talk, incessantly, often, about anything and everything, important or not, Stewart and I fuck our way through this relationship, our time often too short for anything more than physical contact. Sex is how we connect—share our feelings, emotions, and love. I stare back into his eyes, my eyelids closing slightly when he slides one confident finger over the knot of my clit, that finger effortlessly sliding down and into me, the small invasion a tease of perfection. "Look at me," he breathes. "I want to see your eyes."

I reopen my eyes, my mouth parting as he cups my sex, slipping a second finger in with the first, both of them working together, stimulating me in their movement, his thumb staying firm on my clit, soft pressure that moves slightly with each stroke of his fingers. He watches my eyes, sees the moment that the fire of my need hits them, sees the crescendo and burn of my arousal, adjusting the pace and pressure of his fingers in accordance with my want. I feel the curl of pleasure, growing in my belly, our eyes caught in a web of want, pulled to each other, my eyes barely noticing the sexy pull of his mouth into a smile as my breathing increases, and I thrust into his hand. His other hand steals around my waist, sliding up my chest and pulling on the fabric there, tugging my neckline down 'til a breast is exposed, his hand grips and tugs on it just hard enough to make me gasp.

"I want you like this forever," he whispers. "Spread open on my lap, your skin in my hands, your pussy hot and tight around my fingers. You are so fucking beautiful."

I buck under his hand, my heels finding the floor and pushing off, my hand sliding up his pant leg, desperate to feel the heat of him in my hand before I come.

Blackness.

My eyes shut, and I moan, my legs convulsing around his fingers, the strum of his thumb on my clit softening, whisper soft, stretching out my pleasure as I moan over and over again. When it fades, when it softly pulls delicious heat from every area of my body, the need grows. Intense, animalistic desire, a craving for every bit of him in every place on my body. My eyes snap open and find him watching, a curve already in place across that sexy mouth, his hand on his open fly, pulling out the object of my desire and stroking its hard length against my bare leg.

I push his back against the chair, stepping over his leg, straddling his waist and lowering myself down, my sex so wet it drips, my need so great I moan. His hands catch me, carry my ass down, impaling me with his cock, his own groan sounding in the large room, his eyes darkening as I tighten around him. "God, you were made for me."

"I'm your dirty little slut," I whisper, sliding up and down, my heels firm on the ground, his hands tilting and pulling my ass how he likes it, in a way that causes my clit to hit his pelvis, the tight squeeze on my ass pleasurable in its slight bit of pain.

"You *are* my slut," he grounds out. "You need my cock."

"So bad," I agree. "I can't get enough of you."

He thrusts from below, pulling me down, the extra depth causing me to gasp, my body to grind, the pleasure shooting a spike of arousal through my core. "Tell me you love me."

"I love you."

"Again." He thrusts, sitting up, looking into my eyes, our faces inches apart as I look slightly down on him.

"I love you," I whisper, gripping the back of his chair.

Then his eyes close, and he leans back, sliding his hands up and tugging the other side of my dress down, exposing both breasts to his hands. And I know what he wants. I know, just like I know every inch of his body, exactly what he wants. I lean back, my hands resting on his knees, my back arched, my body open before him, and fuck his cock. Pumping up and down on his so-hard-it-will-break shaft, my legs carrying my body, his eyes opening and skimming greedily along my skin, his hand reaching forward and lifting the hem of my dress, strumming the bead of my clit until I come—body tightening, mouth screaming, world exploding.

Then he takes over, leaning forward and scooping me into and against his chest. My legs wrap tight around his body, his cock stiff and slick inside my sex, he carries me over to the wall, presses me up against it, and holds me there with strong arms. Then he thrusts, over and over again, whispering my name softly, and then louder, 'til he comes with a massive groan, his legs shaking beneath him, my own wobbly when he lowers me to my feet. He keeps me there, pinning me against the wall with his body, my breasts tight against his tuxedo, his hands stealing into my hair, his mouth soft and sweet on mine. Drinking from my mouth, tasting me, taking his time, inhaling my scent.

"I missed you this week. I needed that." His voice is gravelly, thick with satisfaction and truth. He tilts my head up, looks into my eyes, then lowers his mouth back to mine.

DELPHINE, W HOTEL

A-FRAME: [NOUN]
LARGE WAVE WITH DISTINCT SHOULDERS
ON THE LEFT AND RIGHT SIDE OF THE PEAK.
CAN RESULT IN TWO SURFERS SURFING
THE SAME WAVE . . . ONE GOING FRONTSIDE
AND THE OTHER GOING BACKSIDE.

Two hours later, my fingers steal under the tablecloth.
Reaching over and gripping Stewart's leg, my fingers deftly
slide up his thigh, his hand catching mine, eyes shooting a
questioning look in my direction. He coughs gently, breaking
eye contact as he glances to the woman on his right. "That's
correct, Beth. With quarterly projections where they're at,
there should be no need for additional debt. If anything, we
should capitalize on our current assets." He listens to her
response, his hand firm on mine, keeping me at bay. But I
need him. I need to feel his strength beneath my hand, to feel
his arousal in my grip. When the conversation turns away
from him, he leans over, plants a soft kiss on my neck, and
whispers in my ear. "Do you need something?"

"Yes. You. Now." It is an unfair request, one I shouldn't make,
but I am panting for him. I will not make it through this four-

hour dinner, through the polite chitchat that will follow, cigars in the men's club while I sit with dignified wives in the front parlor. I need a release, need firm hands digging into my skin, his mouth on mine, cock inside of me.

He studies me, a war going on behind those eyes, his glance flitting around the table and then down at his watch. He leans forward again, close enough that I can smell his scent, the masculinity crawling across the table and robbing me of rational thought. He grips my wrist, pulling my hand tightly and places it on his crotch, brushing his lips against my ear as he speaks. "Call him."

I pull back, confused, his hand cupping the back of my head, keeping me close to him, my eyes studying the tumultuous depths of his blue. "What? Who?"

"*Him*. Call him. Have him take care of you. I can't leave."

There is only one *Him* in our life, our world comprised of three people. I try to process his words, spoken without anger or light, in a serious, I'm-not-fucking-around tone. I shake my head, his eyes sharpening at my reaction, his hand pushing my own down on his cock. His voice rasps in my ear, thick with arousal and authority. "I want it, Madison. I want him to fuck you in the powder room while I sit here with these stuffed shirts. I want you to come back to this table with your cheeks flushed and his cum inside of you."

I feel the twitch of him beneath my hand, see the flicker of excitement in his eyes, and realize the truth of his words. "Seriously?" I whisper, almost afraid to voice the question.

He slides my hand up, letting me feel the hard ridge of his arousal. It is pushing at his pants, his excitement unquestionably hard. "Call him. Now."

I sit there for a moment, the hum of conversation muting as my mind processes this new avenue. My need moans between my legs, its intensity doubled by Stewart's words, by the twitch of him that proved his sincerity. Can I go there? Can I bring these two worlds so close and still escape with our dual relationships intact? I excuse myself and step away, pulling out my phone, watching the dark gleam in Stewart's eyes, a sexy smile crossing his lips. He is serious. He wants me to be fucked while he sits a few rooms away, surrounded by wealth and business. I dial Paul's number, biting my lower lip and step farther away from the table, holding Stewart's gaze.

"Hey babe." Paul's voice is lazy, as if he'd dozed off on the couch.

"Come into town. The W Hotel in Hollywood. I need your cock."

A minute later, I return to the table, smiling demurely at Stewart, who rises at my entrance and pulls out my chair, his napkin hiding any erection he may have. Leaning down as he pushes my chair in, he softly speaks. "Is he coming?"

"There are so many places I could go with that question," I murmur. "But yes."

He sits back down, reaching for his wine glass and smiling at me. "Good."

I try to pay attention to the conversation. Try to eat my salad and smile politely, nod appropriately, laugh when the overweight man to my right makes a joke. But I am waiting, my leg jiggling nervously. Waiting for the buzz of my phone against my leg, for the moment he is here. My call surprised him, his soft voice hardening when he heard my directive. I could imagine him sitting up, trying to put the pieces together, hearing the raw need in my voice. He knows me as well as Stewart does. Knows that when my blood rushes and need hits me, there is only one thing that can satisfy it. Cock. Thrusting roughly, taking my body as its own. He knows I can't contain it, that the need grows and expands until my fingers or someone else's body fucks it to sleep. He knows I won't want to make love. He knows I will need my brains fucked out, and he knows exactly how I like that done. As Stewart does. They have memorized my body, learned my tells, fucked me enough that every movement is delivered before I have to ask.

I am brought back to the present when I hear Stewart speak, his expression calm and intelligent, the rough scrape of his voice only visible to me, who knows it so well. I can see the slight tighten of his jaw, can see the fire in his eyes when he casually glances my way. He is aroused and allows my hand to confirm it when I reach over. Full-blown, hard as a diamond, aroused. It confuses the hell out of me and makes me wet at the same time. Then my phone buzzes, and I am out of time to think. I stand, gripping my purse, waving the men off as they start to rise. "I'm sorry, I'm not feeling well. I'm going to step outside for a bit."

False concern crosses Stewart's features as he rises, excusing himself and escorting me to the door. "You will be the death of me, you know that?" he says softly.

"I could say the same for you."

He stops, outside the door. "Have him fuck you hard," he bites out, pulling me into his body with sudden aggression. "And whatever he doesn't take care of, I will. Just give me a few hours to finish up this business. But hurry." He slaps me on the ass, hard enough to sting, my panties soaked at the forbidden nature of this entire experience. I grip my purse tightly and step out of the restaurant, into the hotel lobby, and head for the restroom.

I knock gently on the unisex door. "It's me." My voice croaks on the last word. This is the closest my two worlds have ever come to colliding. Stewart and Paul. In the same building. My dark and my light. My dark, now seated, surrounded by finery, listening attentively to talks of profit and loss, his cock hard, hidden underneath fine linens and discussions of intellect. And my light, swinging the door open and pulling me inside, slamming it closed behind me and flipping the latch. No words spoken, his hands thrust me back, his mouth greedy on mine as he tastes champagne on my tongue, our need thick in the air. I reach for him, my hand running down his worn tee and grip the top of his jeans. He has not changed clothes since I saw him last, has not dressed up for his entrance into this hotel, and I love the contrast. His messy hair to Stewart's combed. Five o'clock shadow to clean-shaven. The smell of sweat to cologne. I normally get a cleansing period, the twenty-minute drive between my worlds clearing my head, my skin, my palette. Now, walking instantly from one to the other, the comparisons are overwhelming. He pulls back, releasing me. Wiping a hand over his mouth, his eyes take a slow tour of my body.

"Look at you," he whispers. "Dressed up like you are a good girl." He hasn't seen me like this. With my hair conservative and a cocktail dress on, pearls at my neck. He slides my dress up, the expensive fabric stiff, staying where it is put, the black peep of lace panties exposed. I stay still, my back against the wall, legs slightly forward and spread a few feet apart. My chest heaving, need gripping me, I watch him unzip his pants and pull out his cock.

"Suck it. On your knees in this bathroom. Suck my cock while your boyfriend sits at the table."

There is an edge to his voice, an anger that is not normally present. An emotion that turns my easy-going Paul into something darker. *Sexier.* I love it, love the bite in his voice, the possession in his hand as he grips the back of my head and pulls me fully onto his cock. He thrusts into my mouth, his eyes on mine, the connection between us unbroken as he fucks my throat, growing with every pump, the fire in his eyes making the need between my legs almost painful in its intensity.

I pull off him, gasping for breath, his arms pulling me to my feet before I even speak, his arm pinning me to his body as his other hand wraps around, slides underneath the edge of dress and squeezes my ass. Hard. So hard I gasp, his eyes tight on mine and he releases it, running his fingers down the crack of my ass and fingering the channel of my sex, covered in lace. His fingers run back and forth over the spot, a grin stretching across his face at the dampness there.

"Is that for me or him?"

I don't answer, reaching between our bodies and fist his cock, wrapping my hands tightly around it, every vein in the organ outlined in the rigidity of his arousal.

"Answer me, Madd. Answer me while I fuck you right here. While I make you scream so loud that people walking by will hear."

"Make me," I whisper, a challenge in my tone.

His hand tightens around my waist at the words, his eyes holding mine with a fierce look as he listens to my words.

"Make me scream your name while he conducts his business. Make me your slut, right here and now, and send me back to him with your cum dripping out of me."

He groans, pushing me back against the wall, spreading my legs with his knees. He reaches down with both hands, grips my panties and pulls, ripping the sheer fabric with one strong jerk. Then his body is back against me, his chest hard to mine, his bare cock rough and bobbing at my entrance, pushing for and then finding the wetness of my sex and pushing inside. "Jesus Christ, Madd," he groans, shoving upward, his hard thighs pinning me to the wall, his hands yanking at my straps, pulling my cashmere cardigan off my shoulders and jerking the top of my dress down. He thrusts again, his thighs relaxing and then flexing, every fuck bouncing me back against the wall, his hands clasping my breasts, squeezing them into his palms.

"Make me scream," I grit out, my eyes on his. They are tortured blue, cloudy with arousal, latent with need. "You know that he fucked me? Before we came here. I straddled his cock and rode him. His hands rough on my skin, his cock taking my body. He was inside me, Paul, right where you are now." He roars, his voice raw and primal, pushing me against the wall, losing control as he slams against me, faster and faster, until my body becomes a shaking sea of desire, my core rattled, breath gasping, his thrusts urgent and dominant, his breath ragged, his hands finding my face and bringing my mouth to his.

"You are mine," he guts out, pumping into me, the length and level of his arousal brutal. "Mine," he swears, as he releases my mouth and turns me around, pushing me forward as he yanks my legs back, one hand hard on my back, the other gripping my ass. He doesn't slow the movement, giving me full, hard thrusts, my breasts bouncing from the top of my dress, the mirror above the sink giving me a full view of my slutdom.

Paul, in worn jeans, a white t-shirt, light hair mussed, mouth open, intensity over his face. His reflection pulls at my hair, tilting my head back, and I find his eyes on mine in the mirror.

"You like what you see?" His words are terse, thick. He is conflicted, but—from the level of his erection—fully aroused at the same time, his speed increasing, his breath loud in the small space. "You like being fucked while he's in the next room?"

I don't answer, my climax too close, every muscle in my body tightening in anticipation of the act, throbbing and contracting around him, his eyes closing briefly at the sensation.

"God, Madd. You are so fucking good …" He pulls out abruptly, leaving me gasping, my chest aching as I turn to him, feeling his hands before I fully move; they shove me back, wrapping around my waist and lifting me, setting me on the low counter of the sink, and pulling me to the edge. He jacks himself, looking at my pussy, at the swollen pink lips of my sex, then glances up to meet my eyes. He steps forward, pressing himself at my base, pushing my chin up when he sees me glance down. "Look at me. Look at me and tell me what he did to you. Tell me what he did, and make me come all fucking up inside of you."

I close my eyes at his first thrust, the angle different, better, in its brush of my g-spot. "He sat me on his lap, in this same dress. Those panties? The ones you ripped to shreds? I wasn't wearing those when I first saw him. Because I knew he'd take me as soon as he could." He pulls out of me, my eyes catching sight and gluing to the image of my wet lips sliding around his cock. His hands tighten on my ass and he pushes deeper, dragging his cock in and out of me in long, deep strokes. My voice catches at the look in his eyes, the intensity of his arousal. All playfulness is gone. This man before me—he is Stewart, but with different features, their similarities never more present than right now, and I gasp when he fully buries himself inside.

"More," he groans. "Tell me more."

"I came from his fingers, my juices all over his hand, I came and I screamed his name when I did it. I told him how fucking perfect he was and how much he turned me on." His strokes roughened with my words, increasing in speed, his competitiveness lighting a fire in my belly, and I was suddenly there again. On the brink of orgasm, need running through my limbs and pumping loud in my heart. "God, Paul, you have no idea how good his cock feels in me. How deep he goes when I straddle him and fuck him hard. How he whispers my name when I take every inch of him."

He roars, pulling me to the far edge of the sink, thrusting deeper and harder than he ever has, his mouth roughly taking my own, his tongue marking, branding, and drinking from my mouth. I push against his chest, my own body breaking in his arms, the orgasm whirling through me, my words tumbling out as I shudder with pleasure in his arms, his pace never slowing, his cries joining my own, the hot spread of liquid pumped deep with his cock, his name repeated over and over as he finally, with one final shuddering thrust, empties himself inside me.

Five minutes later, I slip back into my seat, Stewart barely pausing in a lengthy explanation of market trends and their expected impact. But I feel his eyes on me, see the casual glance at his watch. "Impressive," he murmurs, tugging my hand to his lips and placing a soft kiss on my knuckle. "I take it you are taken care of?"

I feel drugged, heady with the release and the knowledge of what I have just done. "'Til tonight," I whisper.

"Oh, have no doubt," he says, staring into my eyes. "You will need every bit of energy for it."

I hide a grin behind a long sip of champagne, turning when I feel a soft hand on my arm.

"My wife tells me you sell books," the man says, a polite smile on his face. "Tell me, what authors do you enjoy?"

I smile politely, responding to the man, and feel the rough heat of Stewart's hand, sliding up my dress, and hear his intake of breath when he finds my lack of panties.

We leave the event early, Stewart declining invitations for cigars, blaming my lightheadedness for our early departure. He pulls me by the hand, his steps clipped, my heels skittering to keep up. We push through the lobby doors and into the cool night air, the valet ready with his car, the intense look on his face as he shuts my door sending shivers through my body.

The engine roars as he accelerates out of the garage, his hand fumbling for and unbuckling my seatbelt as he turns onto the road, the traffic light. "I need your fucking mouth on me. Now." He loosely grips my hair and pulls as I bend my torso over the center console, my hands quickly undoing his belt, his erection strong against the expensive fabric.

He grunts when I have it out, my hand gripping it, my mouth on it before he can speak, precum salty and sweet on my tongue, proof of his arousal. His hand pushes my head, pushing me down on it, and he exhales as I take him. "Jesus, Madison." His voice breaks, almost as if on a cry, the need so strong, his hand shaking as he cups the back of my head. "I couldn't fucking think in there. Knowing what you were doing, knowing what you had done. My sweet, fucking girl, full of another man." He thrusts upward on the final word, his sentence ending harshly, thick with competition.

I suck, hard and fast, my hand aiding me, the push and pull of his hand setting the tone, my mouth doing the rest. And it doesn't take long. He is so ready, so primed for me, three hours of buildup turning my steel man into a mess of want and desire. It is gorgeous when he comes.

Gasping my name …
thrusting into my mouth …
twitching, spurting, more and more …
draining down my throat, spilling out around my hand.
I gag, I gulp and he says my name …
over and over …
his thighs flexing beneath me …
his grip tight on my hair.

His car flies into the portico of his building, and he slams on brakes, shoving the car into park, groaning for air as both hands come down on my head, pushing himself up into my mouth for one last thrust, one last drop. Then he pulls me back, lifting under my arms and dragging me across the center, until my dress rides up and my ass is on his cock, his arms encasing me, as I curl into a ball against his hard chest. A chest that is heaving, his heart pounding beneath his skin, his arms wrapping tightly, strongly, around my body. "God …" he whispers. "You are my fucking kryptonite." He leans down, pressing soft kisses on my hair and forehead, his hand releasing me and cradling my face, turning it up to his, before kissing me fully and deeply on the lips. "I love you, Madison. For everything."

And that is how it is. I fuck Stewart, I fuck Paul, and they both know about it. And the more I fuck one, the more turned on the other gets. The more competitive, aggressive, loving they become. It is a constant, whirling sea of sex. I love it, and they love it. They don't need to know who the other is. That would take it a step too close, a step too real. It is better that it is a nameless, faceless individual. And I appreciate keeping the worlds separate. I have fantasies, sure. Of having them both at the same time. Their hands on my body, their competing cocks battling over my skin. But that just seems too messy. And I don't want to do anything to disrupt the perfection that is us. The three of us. Living two separate relationships.

I get that you don't understand—that you wonder how someone could possibly be aroused by the thought of something so forbidden. But often, it is the forbidden that is the hottest, and the depraved that is the most arousing.

DANA

It is unhealthy, this obsession I have with Stewart's love life. Why should it matter who he dates? Why do I care if the blushing blonde on his arm is a flavor of the week or a future wife? I should return to my life, return to my empty condo and my stacks of work. I should not care whether he is happy or lonely, a workaholic or a loving boyfriend. But of course I care. I will always care, I will always love him, and I will always watch out for him. He is my Stewart.

And the blonde from the bookstore—if she is a flavor of the week, she has stretched her flavor into months. Some may call it stalking, some might call it love, but I have continued to watch them from afar. I see her leave his building, her long legs in cutoff shorts and flip-flops, her friendly smile to the valet one of familiarity as she catches the keys and slips into her expensive convertible. I've followed her onto the freeway, the woman driving recklessly, quickly losing me in traffic as I attempt to use a blinker, maintain a safe speed, and not nose dive beneath the tread of an eighteen-wheeler. She is gone, the white car whipping into the glare of the California sun, headed east, my sleuthing attempt a disaster. Except for her tag number. I write it down, with no clear idea of what to do with it.

Maybe he is happy. I hope he is. I called him this afternoon. But again, as it has been for three years, he did not answer.

LUNADA BAY, RANCHO PALOS VERDES

CRUSHER: [NOUN]
SOMEONE WHO SURFS HARD,
AS IF THEY HAVE NOTHING TO LOSE
AND NO FEAR INSIDE.

MADISON

Lunada Bay is Paul's favorite place to surf, waves high and dangerous enough to heat his blood and put a smile on his face. It is also one of the most contested spots to stick your board in. It's located in Rancho Palos Verdes, which is pretty much where all rich white people money goes to die. Colossal mansions sit oceanfront, with manicured lawns and Mercedes that stare out onto waves that kill at least one surfer a year. The local surfers are territorial, running off tourists with sharp voices often backed up by fists, keeping the waves uncluttered and the beach sunbather free. In the '90s, a local television crew was attacked, broken bottles and fists causing blood and bruised egos to scamper back up the slippery slope to the road, their broadcasts interrupted by a trip to the ER. But they allow Paul. They are in awe of him, as am I—his effortless conquer of the waves, his ability, no matter how rough or dangerous a spill, to resurface in the froth. But he wasn't always allowed. I have seen his scar. A long, thick knot of tissue where some spoiled rich kook slashed his side in an attempt to protect this jewel-encrusted strip of beach. Paul returned the next day and battled waves while bleeding through thirty-four stitches. After that, they accepted him as their own, and, when I came into his life, welcomed me with sunburnt smiles.

Today the waves are almost twelve feet. Surfers measure from the back, so a twelve-foot wave is actually, from the shore, twenty-four feet in height, a huge wall of dark water, rising like a beast before curling and crashing onto any surfer foolish or unlucky enough to be in its grasp. I look for Paul, look for his red board, not seeing his head bobbing among the riders. My arms tighten, my eyes scanning slowly, then quickly, my mind trying to recount the last time I saw him.

Then I see his board, a quick rush of relief replaced by nerves. He is out farther, a few hundred yards behind the main peak, at a spot called Truck Drivers. My heart sinks, a heavy weight of doom pulling it down, dragging it to the bottom until it sits somewhere in my stomach, heavy as lead, my breaths coming short and fast.

"Whoa, Paul's taking Truck Drivers?"

I don't turn at the voice, knowing its source. *Rayne*. A dreadlocked Barbie who rarely lifts her head off her boyfriend's cock or the bong he places before her. "Yeah."

"He is crazy, girl."

He *is* crazy. Truck Drivers is a take-off spot for waves, named by some local who had probably died shortly after naming it. It's for daredevils, or anyone stupid enough to want to risk their life for a wave. And the wave that is coming? It is beautiful. Terrifyingly so.

"Uh-oh," Rayne says softly. I don't know whether to slap her or bury my face in her massive chest and avoid the entire thing.

But I can't move. I'm glued to the scene, glued to his form, as he leans forward, lying flat and low on the board and begins paddling, the wave growing larger and more deadly as it develops.

The ocean is a beast. A beast that doesn't care if it chews you up or swallows you whole. A beast you cannot beat—you can only dance with it until the time comes when it kills you. It will never lose, and with moves like this, Paul is living on borrowed time. I watch him paddle and wonder if this is the moment when he will die.

The wall of water raises straight up, sunlight glinting off it in a way that hurts my eyes. I stand, my eyes locked on the one small break in its awesome silhouette, the dip that is my heart, the man I love standing to his feet and disappearing into its churn as it breaks, bending down on itself, Paul's body gone, nothing but white energy before me.

He is, right now, in one of two places. In the channel, hidden by the wave of water, or he's fallen, crushed underwater by the wave.

A breaking wave can push a surfer down twenty to fifty feet, sending them into a washing-machine style spin that tumbles and breaks them apart. When they finally stop spinning, when their chest is breaking apart and fighting against the urge to inhale, they have to regain equilibrium and figure out which way is up. Some surfers swim the wrong way, traveling ten feet before their bursting lungs and their sense of direction alerts them to the deadly mistake. Lack of air is not the only danger. Water pressure at that depth will rupture an eardrum as easily as crushing a fly. Even worse is not having any depth. If the ocean floor, or a reef is present, the wave will grind you against it like a mortar to a stone. Paul *needs* to get to the surface before the next wave hits. The next wave will be a new downward force, a second round in the spin cycle. A second round that compounds the danger, one that his lungs will probably not survive.

Red. Breaking. Far left, shooting out of the front of the curl, Paul's board dipping down and ahead of the break, swinging up, and then down again, his body stepping forward on the nose, arms loose and confident, his movement graceful and relaxed.

I gasp. For him, it was nothing. For me, I just died a small death. I blink back tears and sink to the sand.

"Chocka," Rayne drawls, brushing off her arms and stepping away.

Paul left this afternoon for San Diego, where a tropical storm has created a current he wants to chase. He kissed me quickly, throwing some clothes in a bag and promising to be back tomorrow afternoon unless the weather changes. I am used to it, his excitement over perfect conditions, the unending quest for the perfect wave. A conquer that no one will see, a personal victory only. I watch him leave before dialing Stewart. He doesn't answer, and my texts go unreturned. I mill around the house for a bit, then grab my keys and head into town.

I valet my car and take the elevator up, inserting my key and pressing the button for his suite. Chances are, at eight PM, he'll still be at work. But I can wait, change into comfortable clothes and grab something from the fridge.

Entering the suite, I hear his voice, move down the hall to his office, and step in.

He is on the phone, his face tired, small lines outlining his handsome features. He looks up, surprised, a smile stretching over his face, and he turns in his chair, away from his desk, tapping his thigh, pulling me into his chest when I sit. I stay there for a while, his hand on my back, rubbing as he listens, stopping when he speaks, his other hand scribbling figures on a pad of paper. I can hear the voice in his ear, the phone stuck in the crook of his shoulder, a fast-paced dialogue about product placement, market awareness, and sales trends.

I bore quickly, sliding off his lap, into the opening between his legs, my hand running over his belt, my eyes moving up to catch his. He watches me wordlessly, his eyes urging me to continue, the push of bone under my wrist letting me know he is ready.

He is always ready. His cock seems engineered to spring into action at a moment's notice. It is one of the things I love about him. I unbuckle his pants and stand, pulling my sundress over my head slowly, letting him see every inch of what he will soon get.

STEWART

She is beautiful. I knew that from the moment I first saw her, through snow flurries, a grin on her face like she captured the world and just threw it back. But I didn't really know how beautiful she was until I knew her. Until I saw into her soul and became lost in her goodness. The final step of my capture came when she lost her clothes. Bared her body—that body I see in my dreams, jack off to in the morning, and worship in her presence. And now, with her pulling every inch of that yellow sundress up and off her curves ... I am lost. I am lost, and she has found me. I hang up the phone mid-sentence and unplug the cord from its back.

I roll my chair forward, running my hands along the back of her legs, traveling up the curves of her ass, gripping the skin there as I lean forward and kiss her, tasting the hint of salt that tells me she has been in the ocean. I slide my fingers under the cloth of her underwear, simple pink boy-shorts that I tug down, over the tan curves of her hips, faint strips of paleness showing me her tan lines. Then it hits the floor, and she is bare before me. I start to stand, but she pushes me down, pins me to the chair as she kneels, a playful smile on her face, a gleam of fire in her eyes. I love her eyes. Love how I can instantly tell if she is mad, excited, or in love. Whatever the emotion, whatever her temperature that day, there is always sex in those eyes. It floats off her skin, gleams in her eyes, and is in every move of her delicious body. This woman cannot exist without sex. It is her food, her body-sustaining air. I discovered that early, knew it from our second date. She cannot contain it, does not even try. She embraces it, owns it, loves it. She does not fuck out of insecurity or to get something or someone. She fucks because she loves it and loves through it. It is her gift to the world, and I am lucky enough to be a part of that world.

She feels the strength of my arousal, her smile brilliant in my dim office. Then she unzips me, and I am in her mouth.

Fuck. I will never be able to accurately describe her mouth. It is like a throbbing pulse of wet, hot moisture, seconded only by her body. It knows how hard to suck, how deep to go, how fast or slow to take my cock, and when to give it a moment to regroup. Her eyes flicker to mine, heat in their gaze, and I want nothing more than to pull her to her feet and bend her over my desk. I place my hand at the back of her head, watching in drugged awe as my length slides deeper into her mouth, her pink lips tight around me, the playful gleam in her eyes making my cock harden even further.

I pull back on her hair, trying to lift her up, but she shakes her head, burying me greater, her eyes closing as she gags on my cock. She grips me tightly with her hand, sliding it up and down my shaft, squeezing it, and I feel every bit of stress in my body leave, as if she is milking it out of me. I sigh, leaning back in my chair, content to let her work.

She is beautiful when she sucks a cock. Her cheeks hollowing, the curve of her mouth when she pulls off, the mischievousness in her eyes that telegraphs how much she truly enjoys the act.

I groan, feeling the pressure of buildup. Feeling the push, I'm throbbing in her mouth, close to climax, the three days without her taking their toll on my self-control.

"Fuck baby." I lean forward, cupping the back of her neck, watching intently the movement in and out of her mouth. "Here I come."

She takes me fully, her mouth massaging and squeezing the length of me, my head deep in her throat when I come. Wave after wave of release, my hand unintentionally tightening on her neck, my pleasure audible in the groans I can't contain.

She swallows it all. Her face, when she finally pulls off me—clean—a smile stretching across it. I collapse back in my seat, tugging softly on her skin, pulling her into my arms, her body curling onto my lap. "Thank you, baby. I needed that." I rest my head on hers. "I'm surprised you're here. Thought I wouldn't see you 'til this weekend."

"He had to run down to San Diego. I thought I'd stop by, give you some lovin', stay the night. Maybe kidnap you into a breakfast date."

I frown against her hair. "Can't do breakfast. I have a six AM call with Helsinki."

She tilts her head up, brushes her lips across the rough shadow on my neck. "Then how about I cook you breakfast at five?"

I wrap my arms around her, including her arms and legs in the grip. "That would be perfect. Need me to take care of you?"

She bites my neck lightly. "No baby. Get back to your work. I'll wake you at five." She pushes at my arms, breaking free of my grip and standing, her naked skin glowing in the light from the lamp. I pull at her arm, bringing her closer, getting one last taste of her mouth, before plugging my phone back in and returning to the documents on my desk. As she leaves, tugging the door shut behind her, the phone rings.

ACID DROP: [VERB]
WHEN YOU TAKE OFF ON A WAVE
AND SUDDENLY HAVE THE BOTTOM FALL OUT
AS YOU FREE FALL DOWN THE FACE.

DANA

It is Wednesday night; I am in PJs and socks, a face mask beginning to dry on my face, as I sit in front of the television, popcorn in the microwave. Cross-legged, my back against the edge of my way-too-expensive-but-I-love-it couch, I am flipping through channels, and trying to resist touching my face, to stick my curious fingers into the wet mask, which has not yet fully hardened.

Soap opera. Flip.
Infomercial. Flip.
Football. Flip.
Surfing.

I wait, my remote extended, waiting to see what the show is about, which hotspot or event is being covered. And then I see him, trudging through sand, a board tucked under his arm, that one-in-a-million smile lighting his tan face. My breath catches as I see pure, effortless happiness, no sign of the haunted Paul I remember. Then, there is a blur of blonde, a streak before the camera, a bundle of bikini and cover-up throwing herself into his arms, gripping his neck, and placing a kiss on his cheek. A girl. Maybe she is the reason for his happiness, for the light that shines from his eyes. Or maybe she is a groupie, one of the hundreds of beach Barbies that follow the surfing circuit. I listen to the announcer, to his recount of Paul, of his awards and standings, watching as he swings the girl in a tight circle before setting her down. He pulls her in for a full kiss before she bashfully pushes him away. She turns, and I see her face.

It hurts, the expression I make, the contortion of my face as my jaw drops and eyes open wide, dried edges of the mask pulling and protesting as I stare in shock.

Her.

Tucked under Stewart's arm, their faces beaming as they walked past me in Livello.

A carefree wave to the valet as she left Stewart's world and headed elsewhere.

On her knees, surrounded by books, spewing out friendliness as she gave away lighthearted mysteries.

Her. Stewart's love, the reason for his smile. Hugging Paul. Kissing Paul.

The camera flips to another surfer, and my world blurs, my thoughts moving too quickly for rational thought, question after question pounding through my mind. In the background, the microwave shrills a persistent beep, repeating and repeating, like the countdown timer to a bomb of horrific proportions.

What. The. *Fuck*. Is. Going. On?

MADISON

I enter the bedroom, flipping on the lights and heading for the shower. Twenty minutes later, I crawl into bed and turn on the television. Halfway through a stain-remover infomercial, I fall asleep.

At some point in the night, Stewart joins me, his arms pulling me tight to his body, his mouth soft against the back on my neck. I nestle into his body, murmuring his name, and sleep steals back over me. The next thing I hear is the soft ding of my alarm.

I move half-awake through the motions of cooking. Preheating a skillet. Pouring oil. Beating eggs. The bacon is sizzling in the pan when I lick my fingers and move down the hall, pressing the button next to the light switch that opens the blinds. They move, a soft hum of motors, light peeking through the large windows, the room still dim, dawn on the edge of our city's horizon.

"Wakey wakey," I sing, running my hands lightly through Stewart's hair before planting a soft kiss on his lips. They move beneath my mouth, smiling, and he speaks against my kiss, his eyes still closed.

"It can't be five already."

"It is, baby. I don't joke about interrupting sleep. I've got bacon in the pan, so I've got to get back to the stove." I steal another kiss and then leave, trailing my hands across his bare chest, then jog back to the kitchen, snagging a pair of tongs and turning crispy bacon a moment before it burns.

I have the bacon on a plate and am scooping eggs out when I feel him enter, his heavy presence as palatable as a burst of hot air. I grin, knowing what is coming even before I feel his hands on my ass, gripping and squeezing before sliding his hands around my stomach, coming up and brushing my breasts. He nuzzles my neck. "You can't possibly expect me to eat food when you're naked."

"I'm not naked. I'm almost naked," I protest, slipping out of his hands and carrying our plates to the bar. "Now sit. I didn't get up at 4:30 to have you ignore my breakfast."

He obeys, moving my plate 'til it is next to his and pats the stool. "Well, almost naked, if that is what you call it, looks damn tempting."

"Thank you. You can thank Valentine's Day last year for that."

He tilts his head. "Is that what I got you?"

"And a watch. But I didn't feel like dripping diamonds while flipping bacon."

He grins. "Understandable."

"What's the call with Helsinki about?"

"Rebranding. We're splitting an entity into two parts and need a new brand for the new arm."

Stewart works for a venture capitalist firm. They purchase assets that are typically struggling, then paint a new face on them, streamline their production processes, and use their bulk buying power and outsourcing to reduce costs. Many of his subcontractors are in Finland and India, which makes every hour of the day a business hour. He treats his new assets like children, becoming emotionally invested in their futures, their successes, and their failures. I love his passion, and understand the time commitment and place in his life that his work possesses. In his life, work is first, and I am second. I am okay with that standing, just as he is okay with the fact that I will not make our relationship exclusive as long as I have that second-place ranking.

It doesn't stop me from loving him any less. It doesn't stop my heart from tugging when he smiles. It doesn't stop my recognition that he loves me back, as much as his heart and schedule will allow. I don't want our world to be any different than it is right now. A change in his priorities will mean a change in our relationship. A change in our relationship will mean that I have to choose between him and Paul. And I can't do that. Not right now. I'm not ready for that jump.

He glances at the kitchen clock and bends over, placing a soft kiss on the edge of my lips. "Leave the dishes, babe. Estelle will be here soon. I'm gonna take that call."

I nod. "I'm gonna head back to bed."

And I do. I lose the lace underwire bra and matching thong and crawl back to bed, the motorized blinds dragging the room back into darkness. My heavy breakfast and early morning causes sleep to come quickly, and I don't wake 'til late morning.

The bookstore is busy, a rare occurrence, and the afternoon passes quickly. I sell a grand total of sixty used books, bringing in a whopping hundred bucks. The new books do all right, too, bringing the owner some much-needed revenue and guaranteeing me at least one more month of employment. I lock up at eight, heading next door to the bar that shares our awning.

It is crowded, half tourists and half locals, familiar smiles greeting me as I grab a bar stool. Bip, the bartender, a pretty brunette that has managed to look eighteen for a good ten years longer than physically possible, pops a Corona open and slides it over to me.

"Thanks."

"No sweat, babe. Where's your sexier half?"

"Somewhere on I-5. He's with Nick and Moses, headed back from Del Mar."

"They catch good conditions?"

"According to the text I got, the waves were great, but too many shoobies, so it was a zoo."

"That's the problem with this time of year. Tourists everywhere." She lowered her voice, glancing around before shooting me a smile. "Not that I'm complaining."

"Hey, me either." I toasted her, taking a swig of the beer and glancing at my watch. "Can you put in a large philly to go? I'm gonna head home before it gets too crazy."

Venice Beach has been romanticized by Hollywood and an impressively deceptive tourism marketing campaign. They paint our sidewalk stands and street performers in a romantic light, touting our artistic graffiti and muscle beach as unique oddities. In actuality, it is the armpit of LA tourism. Panhandlers and druggies everywhere, homeless getting rich off intimidated tourists and families of four too far from the safety of their car to say no. We have at least ten murders a year, over three hundred aggravated assaults, and around one hundred rapes. The majority of those crimes happen to tourists, prostitutes, and drug users. Paul and I fall in the lower-risk demographic, but that doesn't mean we are safe. Locals do their best to protect other locals, our misfit band of eccentrics attempting some basic form of civility. But I am a young, attractive female. Walking down the boardwalk after dark alone scares me. I call Paul and let him know I'm on my way home.

"Awesome, babe. I'm twenty minutes away. Gonna drop the boys at their place, and then I'll be home. Call me when you get to the house, so I know you're safe."

I agree, hanging up my cell, and slip it into the pocket of my sweatshirt, the cash tucked away burning my skin. Then I grab my food, throw a twenty on the bar, and head into the crowded night, a half-mile from home.

I move quickly through the crowds, my hood up despite the warm night air, ignoring the catcalls from men and panhandlers who know me yet still stick out their hands. I nod to familiar faces and share words with a few locals. Then the crowds thin, and I am on the sparse path that covers the last quarter-mile home. There are still tourists here, ones who didn't realize that the South Venice parking lot was the wrong place to park, a long walk from the attractions, a much closer lot a quarter-mile north. We all hurry, the night sky unsettling, too many shadows and dark alleys in between the million dollar bungalows that face this oceanfront, broken sidewalk.

Then I reach our street, head a block east and jog up the steps to our home, my key out and ready, the deadbolt flipping in the lock as soon as the door is fully shut. I strip off my sweaty pullover and call Paul.

I hear his jeep rumble as I pull two beers from the fridge, popping their tops and carrying them to the coffee table, flipping the dead bolt switch on my way. He bounds up the steps, flinging the door open and crossing our living room in four easy steps, he pulls me into his arms and takes my mouth. I jump, wrapping my legs around his waist, and he catches me, his hands strong on my ass, his mouth desperate on mine, like he has been away a month instead of a day. He carries me to the couch and tosses me down, the worn leather soft against my back, his mouth following my descent before softly releasing me. His eyes linger on me, a smile on his face before he wheels around and shuts the door.

We eat on the couch, sharing the sandwich, juice running down my wrists as I try to bite into the overfull sandwich. I get up twice for napkins and more beer, our conversation dancing over, but not touching, my activities last night. Paul prefers to not discuss the existence of Stewart. While Stewart approaches their shared split of my time as he would a business merger—coolly and unemotionally—it is much harder for Paul. I have all of Paul's heart, surfing and his career taking a backseat to me, to my happiness. I'm sure he struggles with that—having half of me while giving me all of him. But I was with Stewart first, gave him that half of my heart before Paul ever came into the picture. Paul was just sex to me, a warm body to fuck my body and occupy my days while Stewart worked. But somewhere, over a year ago, Paul took the other half of my heart, and I fell for him as well. I know it bothers Paul. I know he is competitive and possessive and wants me to be only his. But he will not give me up over that desire, so he doesn't fight it. He goes with the flow and only asks for my happiness.

We eat, we watch tv, and then fuck—starting in the shower and taking the activity to our bed. Then we spoon, the sound of waves lulling us to sleep.

DANA

The definition of a secret is something not meant to be known by others.

What do you do when you discover a secret? Do you have a responsibility to share it? Or is the responsibility in the keeping of the secret?

I think it all depends on the outcome of sharing the secret. Some cause harm, some good. I need to find out more about this secret. To know what outcome it harbors. So I will watch. And try to find out as much as I can about this woman. And why she has latched onto these men, who hold my heart as much as she holds theirs.

I don't know if she loves them or is toying with them. The chances of both of us loving them are too slim, too incredible to be a coincidence. What I don't understand is why. Why these two men?

With the millions of men in Los Angeles, why date brothers?

MADISON

I watch Stewart sleep, the rise and fall of his strong chest. He is so rarely still, so rarely calm. Intensity is his standard; peace is a rare moment for me to view. At a time like this, when his eyes are closed and his breathing is soft, I feel protective of him. As if I have some responsibility for his world, for his happiness, for his life. I love him; there has not been a question of that for some time. I fell quickly for this brilliant man—a man who has no time for anything more than quick minutes of affection. He will never bounce our child on his knee or take me to the doctor when I am sick. Those are his limitations, and he realizes that—is regretful for that shortcoming but unwilling to change. He has chosen his lifestyle, and accepts the restrictions that come with it. Maybe one day he will change. Maybe one day his brow will relax, and he will smile easily, laugh more often, and lose the suit and tie. Maybe he will be able to do more than fuck me senseless and kiss me before leaving me alone to sleep. Maybe he will have a life outside of work, and maybe I will still be around when that time comes. Life is too unpredictable to plan for that. What I do know, as I watch this beautiful man sleep, his face relaxed and body still, is that I love him. Just as much as I love Paul. And that, one day, will be a problem.

The fire burned hot, a wave of heat pushing Jennifer Brand back from the pit, her feet sinking in the thick sand. She tripped, stumbling backward, and was caught by strong arms, her gaze looking up and catching on gorgeous green eyes and a cocky smile.

"Gotcha."

She blushed, gripping his forearms and pulled herself to solid sand, brushing off her legs. "Thanks."

"It's Jen, right?"

"Jennifer." She hated Jen, hated the childish lilt of the name.

"Cool. Having fun?"

She nodded enthusiastically, her eyes drawn to his body, to the ripped six-pack he proudly displayed.

"We were actually about to jet. Head to a house party over in Summerset. You seem pretty cool … you wanna come?" He flashed a smile that any warm-blooded teen would be crazy to resist, a grin that displayed his dimples to perfection, his white teeth flashing at her in the dark.

Yes, I would love to come. I would love to do anything your perfect self deems necessary. She hesitated. "I've got to ask my brother, I came here with him."

He stiffened slightly. "Really? Who?"

"Paul Brand."

He stepped back a pace, surprise on his face. "Really? You're Paul's little sister?"

Nodding, she blushed at the impressed look he shot her. "Yeah." It's my birthday … so he brought me along."

His look turned wary. "Eighteenth birthday?"

"Yeah," she lied. "The big one."

He nodded with a smile. "I knew your sister, Dana. You look a little like her. Prettier." He flashed another smile, this one a little awkward, as if he regretted the comment. There was a shout, and he turned, waving absently at a group that passed. "Well … ask your brother. Summerset party. We can drop you wherever when it's done. And tell him I'm a fan. He is lethal on that board."

Stuffing her hands in the front pockets of her jean skirt, she nodded, watching his profile as he turned and jogged through the sand, effortlessly catching a beer that was tossed his way. Then she glanced around, looking for Paul.

He was by the dunes, a blonde head underneath his, his body stretched out over a form she couldn't really see. She hung back, unsure about interrupting, glancing back at the fire before hesitantly calling his name.

There was a groan from the two bodies, and a muffled whisper, then Paul rolled, coming to his feet, his back to her, his hands adjusting the front of his swimsuit before he turned, an irritated expression on his face. "What's up, Jennifer?"

"I'm ready to leave." The words spilled out without premeditation, but she saw the brilliance in them as soon as they came out, Paul's expression fighting hard to disguise the frustration at the statement.

"Now? We haven't even been here an hour."

"I know. There is a big group headed to a house in Summerset to hang out. I could go with them—you could just pick me up there when you're ready to leave here." She said it casually, as if she didn't care either way. As if her entire love life wasn't resting on his answer.

His eyes lit up. "Really. Summerset? Who all's going?"

"Just some girls I've been talking to. But I think it's a big group. So it'll be safe."

The blonde called his name, moving in the sand, and he glanced back before facing her again, indecision in his eyes. "You got a cell on you?"

She rolled her eyes. "Yes. I have Mom's cell, and I'll be with a group. It's just like any other night I go out with a group.

Mom and Dad would be fine with it. Just call me when you leave here. You can pick me up then."

He looked back once more, then studied her face. "All right. Just be safe. I love you."

She grinned, unable to contain the smile that burst out. "I love you, too, Paul. Thanks."

He stepped back, watching her closely. "Cell phone. Don't lose it and make sure the ringer's on. I'll call you in about an hour."

She waved, turning and jogging up the beach toward the fire.

"Happy Birthday!" he called out after her.

She waved again, without looking back, her eyes skimming the fire-lit bodies, looking for the athletic build of her dreams.

He had a football in hand, and was heaving it into the darkness, a dim figure in red jumping up to catch it. She jogged up, tugged gently on his shirt, and waited for him to turn. He did, throwing an arm around her shoulders and pulling her to his chest. "You coming?"

"Yeah. If that's still okay." She beamed up at him.

He squeezed her shoulder gently. "More than okay. Come on, you can ride with me."

He whistled to a group, the guys turning, ditching red cups into the nearby dunes, insults and laughs tossed out as they dispersed.

Five minutes later, she was lifted into the backseat, his strong hands lingering on her waist, his hand sliding the seatbelt across her lap, teasing her bare thighs as it moved. He clinched the buckle, his face close to hers, and leaned forward, pressing his lips against hers as his hand slid around her thigh, caressing the flesh there.

Then he leaned back, breaking their connection, shutting the door and leaning in the open window. "At the party, stick close to me. I'm gonna need more of that."

His words made her smile, her cheeks warm, her lips still tingling from his kiss. "Okay."

He tapped the roof. "Let's go!" he yelled.

She glanced to the boy next to her, extending a shy smile, one that was quickly returned, framed by dark eyes, ruddy cheeks and thick black hair. "Heard you're Brand's sister."

She nodded.

"He's sick on a gun. Everyone knows who he is."

"He taught me how to surf," she offered.

"Hey!" the loud voice from the front seat broke their conversation. "You hitting on my girl, Brian?"

"Just making conversation, Jason," the boy muttered, grinning at her.

My girl. She bit her lip to contain a smile, grabbing the armrest as the truck was slammed into drive, throwing her slightly forward.

DANA

LOS ANGELES GAZETTE
PRESS RELEASE: LOS ANGELES COUNTY

A late night of partying and drinking has taken the lives of three Los Angeles residents, one of them a seventeen-year-old girl. The driver, Jason Tate, is in critical condition at Long Beach Memorial Hospital and had a recorded BAC of 1.23.

Tate's vehicle, a 1992 Land Rover Defender, lost control on Pacific Coast Hwy at approx. 11:14pm on Friday evening. The vehicle crashed through a guardrail before rolling down a steep embank. Jason Tate, a 21-year old UCLA student, was thrown from the vehicle and suffered severe head trauma. The bodies of Brian Jesup and Jennifer Brand were found in the burnt-out vehicle, restrained by seat belts. It is unknown if they were conscious when the vehicle caught fire, the blaze a result of the impact, which cracked the fuselage and tank. The third fatality, Robert McCormick, was found a short distance from the vehicle, and died of head injuries.

A joint memorial service will be held on Saturday at 2pm. In lieu of flowers, please make donations to M.A.D.D. of Los Angeles.

That night ripped apart our lives. I came home, leaving Berkeley mid-semester, and found Mom on her bedroom floor, sobbing, her arms wrapped around a framed photo of our family. One taken before Dad's heart attack. Back when we were a family of six, before we became five, and then four. It wasn't long after that that we became three. Three separate souls, unconnected except for the blood in our veins and love locked away in the stubborn places of our hearts.

"She was seventeen!" Stewart yelled, pushing Paul against the wall, frames rattling against wallpaper from the impact. He dug his hands into Paul's shoulders, their faces only inches apart. "Seventeen!"

"She wanted to go. I didn't know. I thought it was just a party." Paul's words stumbled out of his mouth, a sob thick in the back of his throat, his body slumping down the wall as Stewart released him.

"Did you put her in the truck?" Stewart asked, every word a bite of venom. "Did you look into the eyes of the boy who killed her? Or were you too busy fucking around to worry about something as simple as our little sister's life?"

Paul was silent, his head in his hands, shoulders racking as he tried to contain silent sobs.

"You fucking disgust me," Stewart said, breathing hard, his face tight with barely restrained rage. I left my post by the wall, stepping forward, my eyes meeting Stewart's for a fraction of a second before I wrapped my arms around his chest. He gripped me tightly, so tightly it hurt, his need so great, his heart openly breaking between my arms. "She's gone," he whispered, his voice gravelly. "She's fucking gone." His voice broke, and I felt the shake of him, his strong frame crumbling in my arms, his breath gasping as he buried his face in my hair. "What the fuck are we going to do?"

I held him, my own tears flowing, my eyes blocked from Paul by the wide expanse of Stewart's chest. I wanted to go to him, to hug my little brother, but could feel the anger radiating from Stewart, mixing with his pain, the combination crippling him. I pulled back, looking up into his eyes. "Mom's asking for you."

He nodded, squeezing me one final time before stepping away, his eyes never going to Paul, his profile furious.

I waited until he left the room, pulling the door shut with a finality that hurt, then hurried to Paul, crouching down next to him. I wrapped my arms around him, shushing him as I felt him shake. When he moved, sitting up against the wall, his wet eyes staring straight ahead. I curved into him, his arms automatically moving around my shoulders, taking me into his embrace. "He hates me," he whispered.

"He's just in pain," I said softly. "He'll change, Paul. He knows you were just trying to do the right thing."

"I wasn't. I was being fucking selfish," he choked out. "I should have been with her. It was her night. It's my fucking fault." He tightened his arms around me and rested his head on mine, letting out a shuddering breath. "It's my fucking fault, and he knows it. He *should* hate me."

"He doesn't hate you. He loves you." I said the words and believed them to be true. But Stewart may have loved Jennifer more. And when one love kills another, can you still love the one who's left?

Stewart left minutes after the funeral ended. He and Paul didn't see each other for three years—until Mom's funeral. They framed her casket, two visions of handsome in black suits with somber faces. Then the separation continued. It has been seven years and three months since her death. Over seven years of silence.

The first few years, I ran ragged between the two of them. Attempting reconciliations. Planning peace-keeping holidays, birthdays, lunches. But the time only increased the distance, and after two years of trying, Paul asked me to stay away. Said that it was too painful to see my face. Said I reminded him too much of her. I fought it, continued to try. Then he changed his number, moved. Made his feelings crystal clear.

I hope that now, as an adult, Paul realizes the implications of his actions, but also the reality of the true cause. Stewart buried him so deep in guilt that it took years for him to smile again, to realize he is a good person who made a simple mistake. I think he now begrudges Stewart for those years of pain, when he was close to suicide over the loss of his sister and the overwhelming guilt he felt.

But Stewart … he still blames Paul for her death. And he is too proud to admit anything to the contrary.

They both loved her. So much. Almost too much. So much that her death was impossible to recover from, at least where their relationship was concerned.

And that brings me to the present. Another woman holds both of their hearts in her hands. Their relationship didn't survive Jennifer. I'm worried their hearts won't survive Madison. I *have* to protect them. I am their sister. It is my duty.

MADISON

The alarm chirps in our silent bedroom, soft yet insistent, my mind swimming through remnants of a dream as my hazy mind deciphers sleep from reality. I hear Paul groan, feel the bed shift as he rolls over, the knock and roll of bedside table items, and then silence. I open my eyes briefly to dawn light, and try to figure out what, where, and why the alarm would be going off.

Ugh. It comes to me, reality waking me with a cheerful smack on the head. Mother. I sit up, my brain momentarily gripping my skull, a painful reminder of what late night poker, cigar smoke, and too much Miller Lite can do to your head. Paul rolls over, reaching for me, and I lean down, ignoring the scream of pain in my head, and kiss his forehead. "Go back to sleep. I've got brunch with Mom."

"Have fun."

I playfully bite his earlobe, harder than is necessary, and he yelps, pulling the covers over his head and pushing me off. I head to the kitchen, bee-lining for aspirin and water.

Mother. I prepare myself as I drive, for the inquisition that awaits me. Even though she has foiled most of her adult life, she still considers herself the foremost authority on my life, and will spend every moment of the upcoming event to make sure that my life is on the proper track. Parental guidance doused in bourbon.

I enter the curving hills of Rancho Santa Fe a half-hour ahead of schedule, my convertible slowly winding through the familiar roads of my childhood. I have a brief moment of nostalgia for my diamond-encrusted upbringing, familiar homes and restaurants reminding me of shopping, teenage groping over the gearshifts of Ferraris, and spring break trips to Europe. I turn into the large gates of Maurice's neighborhood and roll down my window.

"May I help you?" This neighborhood doesn't believe in rent-a-cops. They employ off-duty police officers, give them crash courses in overkill, and then post them, like sentries, outside of million dollar gates.

"I'm here to visit Evelyn Fulton. My name is Madison Decater." I pull out my identification, passing it to him, and ignore the death stare he seems intent on sending my way. He checks my trunk, a miniscule space barely big enough to hold a case of beer. Then we go through the song and dance where he quizzes me, verifying that I, in fact, know my mother's address, that I am not staying for longer than four hours, and that Maurice and Mother are expecting my arrival. It's a good thing I am ahead of schedule. Heaven forbid I miss a moment of brunch.

The gates finally open, the guard fixing me with a glare of the Bruce Lesnar variety, and I wave cheerily, cranking up the radio and pulling forward with a gentle squeal of tires. Five minutes later, I am lost.

Fuck. I stare at the giant Mediterranean villa before me. All of these homes look alike. Huge. Tile roofs. Palm trees. Dollar signs. When one home got a private gated entrance, they all did, the constant need to one-up each other steamrolling into a giant ball of *allourhouseslookthesame.* I have only been here a handful of times, my avoidance of Mother's new life a dedicated one. It's been six months since my last examination from that security guard, long enough to smear my compass and flush my memory of intelligent, directional thought.

I repeat the address in my head, reversing the car and looking for a street sign, some indicator of which part of Posh I inhabit. Nothing. This ridiculous excuse for a neighborhood doesn't believe in street signs or house numbers, something so ghastly as numerical digits having no place in their architectural façade.

I glance in my review mirror, terrified that flashing lights and an overzealous cop man will appear and start another round of questioning. I plug the address into my car's GPS; it, and my iPhone's map informing me that I am, technically, in the middle of nothing, a blue dot in the midst of brown dirt. Apparently rich people privacy includes exclusion from modern directional satellites. I grit my teeth and call Mother's cell.

"You're late."

"I'm lost. You're neighborhood refuses to make any helpful overtures when it comes to directing strangers."

She sighed. "Where are you?"

I look at the house before me, barely visible behind the large gate and landscaped foliage. Then pull slightly forward, to a slightly different gate, with another well-hidden home. "I see gates. Big ass gates and little bits of home."

"Watch your language, Madison. I did raise you to be a lady."

I avoid that conversational landmine, driving farther, until I see a house that is actually visible, behind yet another imposing iron gate. "I'm in front of a white house. Spanish style, with an orange tile roof."

She huffs impatiently into the phone. "You know, the food is getting cold. And I don't have every home in this neighborhood memorized. Our house faces west, and we are in the back of the neighborhood. I'll send one of the help down to stand by the gate."

The help. I bite back a response, schooling my brain as my mouth opens. "Thanks, Mom. I'll be there soon." Movement catches my eye as I end the call, and a white SUV pulls up behind me, its roof flashing red and white. I let out a groan, watching the door open and a uniform emerge.

RANCHO SANTA FE, CA

I watch my mother carefully. Watch the slight tremor in her hand as she reaches for her drink. Watches the polite smiles she gives her husband—smiles one would give an acquaintance, not a loved one.

I don't mind Maurice. In terms of a husband, she could have done worse. He is polite, respectful, puts her on a pedestal her beauty dictates but her behavior doesn't deserve. He belongs to the proper clubs, has the acceptable nine-figure balance sheet, and gives her complete freedom, not that she uses it for anything other than drinking.

But he's ancient. Oxygen-mask, Depends stuffed in his nurse's apron, might-not-make-it-to-Christmas ancient. And Mother, despite the tremor in her voice, and her inability to do anything other than mourn her past life, is beautiful. Half natural-beauty, half enhanced by the team of world-class plastic surgeons who she has employed her entire life. She looks thirty-five, with smooth skin, cosmetically perfect bone structure, and a body that most twenty year olds would kill to have, myself included. I don't know why she fights so hard to keep up her appearance, since she never leaves this house, never visits the country clubs they belong to, or the restaurants they could buy ten times over. Her friends all abandoned her around the time our money ran out. I think she thought when marrying Maurice they would all come back. Welcome her into their perfect little fold. But she was tainted, their blue blood unable to forget her fall from grace, her drunken wander through the Spring Charity Gala, our home, with overgrown grass and no housekeeper. Her daughter's exclusion from the debutante ball. They had seen her weakness, and wanted no part of her return, despite the new wardrobe and prestigious address that accompanied it.

"Have you given any thought to returning to school?" Mother's voice interrupts my depressing walk down memory lane, her eyes cutting me from across fourteen feet of fine dining.

"No." Short and sweet is the best approach with her. It is likely she won't remember this meal tomorrow.

"And why not?"

"I have a job, Mother. I am doing just fine."

"Still single?" she asks, her perfectly waxed eyebrow raised.

My relationship status is her gauge of my personal success. With a wealthy boyfriend, of husband potential, she'll cross me off her 'things to worry about' list, however short it may be. In her mind, a man is all I need. Someone to take care of me. Whether or not love is involved is a moot point.

"Yes, Mom. Still single."

I'm not going to go into my dual relationship status with her. Not in front of Maurice, and not when our mother-daughter chats are spread six months apart. It's easier to listen to her lecture me about my singleness than hear the reaction that the truth would cause. And if I only told her about one, then she'd want to meet him, would probably surprise me in Venice, clad in Chanel, ready to play Dutiful Mother for an afternoon before being driven back to her alcohol-infused life.

"Do you need money?"

Her eyes have noticed my car. The clean lines of my clothing, the Chanel J12 watch that decorates my wrist. She knows I don't need money, but I think the offer makes her feel superior. It is proof she has succeeded. Pulled her life together and risen from the ashes of my father's crash. "I don't need money, Mom. I'm good."

Maurice interrupts our awkward exchange, asking about books, and our lunch takes a pleasant turn, discussing the latest bestsellers and our thoughts on them. Maurice is a reader, his library one that I would get on my knees and suck dick for. I'm talking fourteen-foot ceilings, worn paperbacks and hardbacks filling deep bookshelves that take up three walls and reach to the ceiling. I've spent hours curled into the deep leather chairs in front of the fireplace, a stack of books before me. It is where I escape during holidays, parties, and any other occasion that dictates my presence in this household.

After the table is cleared and Mother switches from mimosas to Arnold Palmers, I help Maurice to his feet, and we make the long and slow journey to the library. I've brought a stack of new hardcovers—knowing his taste in reading. We sit down before the fireplace, and I walk him through the selection, stacking them in the order that I think he'd prefer.

Then we read, in companionable silence, for two hours, until I notice the time and stand to leave. I walk over to Maurice, who has fallen asleep, his head tilted back at an awkward angle, and I gently place a small pillow under his head and lightly kiss his cheek. Love is a strong verb for my feelings for him, appreciate a more accurate term. I appreciate that my mother has someone to take care of her, even if I don't understand the dynamics of their relationship, or what it is that he gets from her. I think, at a certain age, loneliness is the biggest battle to fight, and I hope my mother, in her inebriated state, at least provides companionship for him.

I find my mom in the front parlor, sitting back in a chair, also asleep. I set a book next to her, the last one in my bag, a romance I know she'll enjoy. I head for the front door and smile at the uniformed girl who holds out my jacket. "Thank you. Please thank them for the brunch."

She nods politely and opens the door for me. I take one last glance at my mother and then step out, the cool spring air reminding me of the jacket in my arms. I shrug into it and jog down the steps down to my car, ready to get back home.

Life in luxury can be stifling.

I walk into our home, greeted by the delicious view Paul's backside, a wet suit unzipped and hanging from his hips, baring his upper body, hiding his bottom half in skintight vinyl. He turns, a bowl of what smells like Kraft Mac & Cheese in his hand, a spoon halfway to his mouth.

"Back so soon?" he asks me through a mouthful of food, setting the bowl on the counter and stepping over, wrapping a hand around my waist and pulling me tight to his hard, wet body.

I resist the urge to push him off, the damp feel of him sinking through my clothes, the scent of salt water hitting my nose. "It was a quick visit—one to appease my mom before their trip to Italy." I smile up at him, his hand gripping me tighter, and as he presses me against him. I feel an entirely different type of hard muscle. My smile widens, and I laugh, dropping my bag on the floor and wrapping my arms around his neck. "God, you are impossible."

"What can I say? I'm addicted." His words are soft, so sweet and sincere that they tug my heart in a way that cannot be described. I reach between us and tug on the zipper of his suit, dragging it down, his breath increasing, ragged against my mouth as he releases my waist and grips my face, pulling it to his with both hands. He walks me backward until I hit the counter.

I cup him in my hand, pulling him out, the weight and rigidity of him beautiful, causing a weight in my pussy, a need in my core. His mouth softens against me and he takes his time, dipping slowly into my mouth as he thrusts forward with his hips, begging me for more with his body, his cock sliding in and out of my hand, slick vinyl cool and itchy against my thighs.

"You're wet," I whisper, coming off his mouth.

"So are you," he replies, pressing forward, pinning me against the wall as he takes another taste of my mouth.

It is a fact I can't deny, my panties sticking to me, his hands reaching down and pulling up my dress, the thin material contrasting with the cashmere sweater that I wear over it. I move his cock, placing it between my legs, my boots putting me at a height that makes us fit perfectly together, the warm space between my legs squeezing his cock, the slow in and out of his bare thrusts creating a delicious friction between my legs. "I love you," he says, tucking my hair behind an ear and staring into my face, my eyes closing as the slide of his cock draws a long pull of pleasure against my clit. "I need you."

"I need you, too. Right fucking now." I open my eyes, catching the full brute of his ocean-blue eyes, the skin around them tan despite the cool air, flecks of gold in his hair, bleach blond brows furrowing as he squeezes my cheeks, pulling my pelvis tight to him, the fit of us causing his breath to hiss.

"As you wish," he growls, lifting up with his hands, my legs leaving the floor, a shriek of surprise escaping my mouth. He kneels, with me in his arms, lowering me to the kitchen floor. Setting me gently on my back, the hard floor cushioned by my sweater, his hands pull my skirt up and slide my panties to the side, a finger slipping into me, his eyes lighting up at the touch.

Then he is inside me, fucking me on the floor, our legs a tangled mess of boots and bare feet, his wetsuit wreaking havoc against my legs, but I don't care. I don't care about anything other than the perfect, slick pattern he is fucking into me. His face stares down at me, framed by the flex and pull of his shoulder and chest muscles as he takes me with his cock.

It is fast, it is messy, our bodies bouncing in unrestrained passion, his breath hard on my skin, his hands bracing against the floor, the deep thrusts that cause me to wrap my legs around him and gasp with every stroke.

He rolls, keeping me inside of him, my sweater now hot, and I yank it off, my arms tangling in it, his hands helping to pull it free. I grin, his playful smile matching my own, his length twitching inside of me, a subtle hint for me to move. I lean forward, resting my hands on his chest and ride, up and down, each downward pump grinding my pelvis against him, his hands running lightly over my breasts, his eyes glued to mine. I fuck him until I come, crying out as I clench him tight and sink onto his chest. He takes over, pumping his cock up into me, holding me tight with his arms, his mouth hot on my neck, my body stilling as he hammers out swift fucks.

Then he comes. *I love to hear him come.* He is vocal, moaning my name as he thrusts hard and deep, his arms tight around my body, his actions almost frantic in their movements. He needs me. He loves me.

He stills his hips, his arms reaching up and pulling my hair to one side, his mouth soft against my skin as he kisses my collarbone. I close my eyes, enjoying the trail of his fingers against my skin, his cock getting soft inside me, the cool air from the open window floating over my bare ass. I love him. I need him, too.

My relationship with Stewart is a catch 22. If he didn't work, or didn't have a slave's addiction to the work, our relationship would be a success. We would have the fabulous sex life, and the relationship to accompany it. We would drink champagne in bed and share our hopes and dreams, stories of our past. We would spend weekends in bed and drive to the beach when the sun was out. We would have children and watch them grow up, argue over bedtimes and house rules. All that is not possible because of the full-time mistress that is his job. But if he weren't married to his work, if he was a normal man with free time and a clear mind, then he wouldn't be my Stewart. He wouldn't have the same intensity, the confidence and satisfaction that he gets from his job. He is the job. His entire being, the traits that I love, are all cultivated and created on that phone through deals and negotiations. Stewart without his single-minded devotion to work … I wouldn't even know that man. He would be a stranger to me. And if I had a full-time Stewart, then I wouldn't have Paul. A full-time Stewart would have no reason, no need for Paul. A full-time Stewart would want me all for his own.

He wakes me with his mouth, interrupting a dream with a reality far sweeter. His mouth awakens my passions as well as my body, and he claims me, sliding his warm body atop mine, nudging my knees apart and grinding his body against me, the smooth slide of naked skin causing me to shiver beneath him. His cock grows hard between our bodies, and we are both ready when it bumps lower, thrusting inside of me.

It is the perfect way to wake up, the perfect way to start my day. Stewart knows what I need, knows the insatiable pull within me. And, wrapping my arms around his neck, I let him fulfill me.

Fourteen hours later, he drives, his hand loose on the gearshift, the car taking the tight curves of the road with ease. He drives like he does everything else: intently, with an edge of recklessness barely restrained by tight control.

I lean back, letting my head drop against the headrest and run my hands gently over his forearm. He is happy, his mouth turning up at the edges, a secret grin playing over his features. His hand releases the shifter and turns up, my palm sliding into his and our fingers interlock.

He won't tell me where we're going. Just waltzed in the condo, catching me mid-bite on the white leather couch in the foyer, the couch I'm not supposed to eat near, a Dorito filling up my mouth, Coke balanced precariously on the sofa's arm. He shot the soda a bemused glance and reached out, grabbing my hand and pulling me to my feet, the bag of Doritos dropping to the floor. "I want to show you something."

And now we are driving. Out of downtown, taking the freeway east, toward the ocean. I crack the window slightly and let a burst of fresh air inside, Stewart promptly rolling the window back up. I sigh, watching as the exterior stills and the car makes a slow turn into a residential area.

"Are we visiting someone?" Stewart and I don't socialize outside of business functions. We don't have friends or acquaintances. We exist, in our own bubble of two, our time too short to waste making small chat with strangers.

"Just be patient." He pulls out his phone, checks an email, then looks up. "Look for Palm Drive." The car slows, and he rolls both windows down, squinting into the darkness.

"Right there." I point ahead. "To the left."

We turn, he looks at his phone again, and then we make the final, undercarriage-scraping turn into the driveway of a one-story bungalow, Spanish-style white, blue shutters framing its front windows. He puts the car in park, and I wait, confused, glancing out at the dark house, no lights on inside. An empty driveway.

"Let's go in." He unbuckles his seat belt and opens the door.

We step into darkness, the front door opens with a key Stewart produces from his pocket. He walks through, leaving me in the foyer, lights flipping on as he moves, illuminating marble floors, a chef's kitchen, a fireplace built into the far wall. My sense of unease grows until he finally reappears, standing before me and spreading his arms proudly. "So? What do you think?"

I step toward him, glancing around. "I'm a little confused. Are you moving?" I know he's not. He can't. The ten-minute commute would drive him crazy—thousands wasted in those precious minutes spent on something as trivial as transportation.

"It's for you." His smile falters slightly at my expression. "Don't you like it?"

"But I already have a house." *With Paul.* The words that don't need to be said.

"You *rent* a house. In a section of town that has the crime rate of Compton." His tone irritates me.

"I *like* where I live." *And whom I live with.* Paul would move, but only to make me happy. He wouldn't *want* to live in this manicured neighborhood of picket fences and paved drives. Twenty minutes from the water, from our lives as we know it. "I'm right by work now."

"You'd be closer to me here. And this is nicer, ten times nicer than where you live." He is right, though he has never been to my house. For all he knows, it has twelve-foot ceilings and five bathrooms.

I try to breathe, try to stay calm. "Have you closed on this?"

"No. It's closing in ten days. Sooner if you'd like."

No. I would not like. "Stewart, this is a very kind gesture, and I really appreciate the thought ..."

"But you don't want to move." His face is unreadable, and I step forward, wrapping my hands around his neck.

"No. I don't want to move. Can you pull out of the sale?"

He sighs, his hands sliding around my waist, slipping under the top of my jeans, and he squeezes the skin there. "It's gonna be hard." He pulls me forward, pressing the length of my body against him, my breath catching as he lifts up with his hands, pulling me tight to his pelvis.

"How hard?" I breathe.

His mouth curves beneath my lips and he leans forward, taking a deep taste of my mouth before pulling off. "Why don't you get on your knees and find out?"

I think it hurt his feelings, my refusal of his gift. But it was too much. Not the gift of the house—I'm not too proud to accept a million dollar piece of real estate. But the life change. I love my time with Stewart. But the everyday with Paul? Waking up next to his warmth in the house that creaks under our feet and has hosted our sex in every counter, bathroom, and floorboard? I love that part of my life. And all of it would change if we were to move into a house of Stewart's. The entire dynamic of our lives.

Sex smoothens his hurt. Sex heals his ego, and he earns every ounce of it back. Making me scream his name, my body bent over, gripping the granite countertop, his hard cock claiming me from behind. On my back in the master, my legs spread before him, his hands lingering over my skin as he fucked me to a second, then—legs flipped over and my body on its side—third orgasm. We finished on the back deck, the night air cool on our hot skin, his breath labored as he kissed the length of my skin, his hands following his mouth, making a final exploration of my body, pushing me down to my knees.

We christen the hell outta the house, despite my lack of future inside it. Then we turn out the lights and Stewart locks the door with one last, regretful look inside. "You sure you don't want to sleep on it? Ashley will be so disappointed, she thought you'd love it."

"Then you can buy it for her," I tease. "But no."

He turns the key, snagging my arm as I turn, and presses me against the door, taking one more possessive, full-body taste, his mouth aggressive as his hands take a long survey of my body. When he finally releases me, I stay against the door, looking up into his face, partially in shadow, his looks no less devastating in the dark. "Thanks, baby. For thinking of me."

"I love you. I want you to be taken care of."

I smile. "I am. I don't need a house for that." I stick out my tongue playfully, and the serious moment is broken. He tugs at my hand, and we return to his car. And then to his condo. Which we christen also—just for the hell of it.

A normal person would ask themselves who they prefer. If both men were standing on a cliff, and I had to push one of them off, who would it be?

But I'm not normal, and neither are they. Eventually, one of them will tire of this relationship—will want more. Will want a full-time girlfriend or mother to his children. And then I will ask myself if that is what I want. If I can be happy with one man. And if the answer is yes, then I will go that path. It seems strange but, despite their differences, there is a bit of each other in these men. And even if I leave one, I will always have part of him in the other.

Paul knows that one day that question will come, and he avoids it—will never bring that question to my attention. Stewart doesn't have time to think about it.

VENICE BEACH, CA

DIDDY MOW: [NOUN]
THE WORST KIND OF WIPEOUT.
ONE THAT CAUSES BROKEN BONES, MISSING TEETH,
OR LOSS OF LIFE

It's one of those barely warm days. The kind that warns you to get out and enjoy the water before it is teeth-chattering cold, with breezes that feel like the open door to a fridge. I close the windows in the house this morning. Crawl back into bed and lay on Paul's warm body. Let him wrap his arms around me and warm my skin.

We wait 'til noon, when the sun has been out long enough to take the chill off the day, and then run out, the initial shock of cold water goosebumping our exposed skin. After an hour our muscles are warm, and we are contemplating the incoming waves.

I love the anonymity of being out here. The sand and water don't care if you are a spoiled rich kid or a foster child. It doesn't yield to society's expectations or discriminate. And there is little you can buy that will improve your ride of a wave, or lower your risk of death. On the sand, in the water, we are all equal in the wave's eyes. All opponents that will either conquer the surf or succumb to it.

I rode a surfboard before I ever did a bike. The waxed feel of epoxy underneath my soles is as familiar as sand. I am not Paul. I don't ride on the edge of death, don't tackle the monsters that rise above and crush down on innocent souls. I ride the waves I know I can handle and don't bite off more than I can easily chew. And this, this gradual curve that approaches, is a wave I can handle.

I watch it coming, feel the tug as it pulls from behind me, the subtle awakening of the surrounding water as we all prepare for its arrival. I glance around, Paul nodding, sitting up and gesturing for me to go, no other surfers around. A collision on a wave is dangerous, the hard impact of boards brutal at a time when the smallest mistake can mean danger.

I count the seconds, watching the curve of ocean, feeling the pull of current, and then lean forward, lying flat against the board, and paddle. Quick, strong strokes, the rush of excitement entering my muscles as I pick up speed. It is coming. I am ready.

PAUL

I love her. She knows it. I don't hide the fact. But I don't think she knows how *much* I love her. How my chest expands to a point of pain when she smiles. How I ache when I leave her, how my hands shake when I finally get to touch her again. She is everything I don't deserve and everything I could ever hope to attain. I watch her, the glint of sun off her hair, her blue wet suit bending as she leans forward, her feet swinging onto the board, and her movement as she paddles away from me.

Her hair is loose, long, wet, blonde tendrils, falling off her shoulders, her yellow board cutting through the water. The wave lifts me, coming in strong, my feet pushed and pulled as it moves by. I frown, not liking the kick of water that spins beneath my feet. It is stronger than it looked, catching me off guard. I narrow my eyes and watch her form, her graceful leap onto the board, her arms steadying out. My angel.

I see her form rise and fall, and then she is gone, hidden by the curve of the wave.

MADISON

The board vibrates under my feet as I move forward, getting my footing and balancing, my arms outstretched, legs bent. I hit my spot and feel the lift of the board. I lean a little right, the board responding, and we hit the swell and slide down, gliding along the surface, picking up speed, my hair whipping in front of my eyes, stinging my face. I bend slightly, resisting the urge to tuck my hair back, every movement on a board attached to consequences. Then we tilt, the entire world, the wave stronger, faster, than I had expected, and the board shoots from underneath my feet, and I am yanked by my ankle strap, my feet flying outward. Unforgiving water smacks hard against my back and I am yanked underneath, my mouth opening, a stolen breath captured before I am engulfed by ice cold water.

White noise.

The current is strong, unexpectedly so, and I tumble, pulled underwater, my eyes blinking rapidly as I am tossed around—the rough push and pull of water disorienting me, my struggle against the current useless. My lungs are beginning to burn, panic setting in, my foot pulled by my leash, and I hope to God it is pulling me toward the surface. The board should float, that should be the direction up. But my body is caught in a rip current, and I fight it, kicking and clawing, black spots appearing in my vision, my lungs stretching and bursting in my chest. My hand breaks into air, and I kick hard, my foot unexpectedly free, and suddenly I have too much to process and not enough oxygen to react.

I realize it all a second too late. A second before my face hits the surface, fins come slicing through the water, the yellow flash of my board, rubber-banding back, the pressing against the leash too great, its recoil effect headed directly toward me.

Impact.

PAUL

I cannot see her. The wave came, she stood, she rode, and then she fell. We all fall. I fall into five-foot monsters, the kind that eat up and spit out surfers like gum. It is okay. She knows how to fall, knows what to do if the current pulls her under. Knows to go limp and let it spit her out. But this one had a strong kick. I felt its pull, worried over its strength. But still. She will find the surface. I will see her bright yellow board, her mess of sunlit hair. I paddle forward hard, my eyes skimming, another wave coming, its back draw pulling me briefly away. Then there is a flash of yellow. Her board, bobbing to the surface. I pause, searching carefully, then frantically, for a sign of her body.

Dark blue expanse, occasionally dotted by colorful bits of surfer. White foam, dark seaweed, her yellow board. Nothing else. Dark blue expanse.

Then I see her suit, bubbling to the surface, facedown in the water, and my entire world ends.

I fly through the water, added by waves, at her board in seconds, my hands flipping her over, her body moving easily, without resistance. Without life. I pull her onto my board, bending down, undoing the velcro of her ankle leash, hesitating as I hold the cord. She will kill me if her board is lost. It is an extension of her, of her life on the water. We have fucked on these boards, kissed, slept on the water, and fought the demons in these waves. Then I push it aside and lean over her body. I pump at her chest, I breathe into her mouth, and I look to shore and wonder if I should paddle in.

It is a horrific decision to make. To continue working to save her life, or to take her somewhere where she might need to be. The shore holds paramedics, defibrillators, oxygen. Shore means at least two minutes of paddling. Maybe longer, my speed hampered by her additional weight on the board. I pray to a God I have ignored for too long and exhale into her still mouth.

The first time I kissed her was on the roller coaster. Hard plastic underneath me, the scent of sunscreen coming off her skin, she had reached over and pulled me to her like it was nothing. Like it was natural that we would spend that moment, as strangers, exploring each other's mouth. She had been so gorgeous, so vibrant. It was like she had been pumped so full of life that it was spilling out; she overflowed with it. Just being with her, in line, on that ride, her hand in mine... it was intoxicating. That kiss was my first injection, and she became my addiction from that point forward. Addiction made me come back after she told me about the other man. When she shared that I would be one of two, owning only half of her heart. I worked it out then, and I don't care now. I only need her in my life. The rest can be made to work.

It isn't working. I push against her chest harder, the wet suit slick beneath my palms, my movement awkward on the thin board, a large wave knocking me off balance when I lift from her chest. I look to shore and lay down, as gently as I can, atop her body, and paddle as fast as my arms will go.

I have paddled hundreds of miles. Accelerated bursts of speed to catch up to a wave. Long sprints to race another surfer back to shore. But never has my stick moved this fast. I gasp for air, my heart squeezing in my chest as I move my arms, listening, straining my body for a hope of air, a movement in her limbs, a sigh. *Something.* I try to calculate time, to know how long it has been, but panic sets in, and I push those thoughts to the side. I notice the blood halfway to shore. Beads of liquid streaming down the board, coming from her head. *Do the dead bleed?* I scream, the shore approaching, and heads look up. Feet move along the sand toward us, and I clear the final distance 'til it is shallow enough to stand, and I sweep her cold body into my arms.

Her lips are blue. Her face is slack. I have failed her. I hold her tight to my chest and run out of the water.

HACK SHACK: (NOUN)
HOSPITAL

PAUL

I have only ever loved four women in my life. The first two are dead. I have lost communication with my sister. I am praying fervently for Madd. The paramedics surround her, their red polo-adorned bodies bent over, voices crawling over each other, and all I can see are her feet, sticking out, pointing to the sky, in a way I have never seen them. She curls into a ball when she sleeps, her feet tucked, her head often on my stomach or my arm, her mouth curved into a smile even when she is sound asleep. They push me aside, won't let me close enough to see, but I can hear their words. There is a siren in the distance, and all I can do is thank God that we are in Venice. Where there is medical staff on the beach, ambulances around the corner. Not up in Lunada or out in Malibu where empty mansions would quietly watch her die.

There is a cough, and my heart leaps. More coughs. Hard, hacking sounds that she has never made, the type of sound that must come from a grown man. Her foot moves, and I pray it is her movement, and a medic didn't bump it. An engine rumbles, and I am pushed aside once again as an ambulance pulls onto the sand. The last thing I see is her limp feet as she is placed on a stretcher. They won't load a dead person onto a stretcher, won't send them in an ambulance.

Right?

I get the attention of an EMT, grabbing his arm when he shuts the ambulance doors. "I'm her boyfriend. Can I ride with you?"

The man turns, his thin face looking me briefly up and down. "They won't let you in the hospital without a shirt and shoes. We're taking her to Venice Regional. Why don't you grab some clothes for you and her? Just in case. Also, if she has any identification, numbers of friends and family ... grab that type of thing and meet us there." He moves around me and opens the passenger door. I turn, my feet slipping on the hot sand, and run. Past familiar faces, past a dread-headed stranger who is examining my board, jumping over a handrail, my feet pounding a path that I have taken many times before. With Madd and without her. I round the corner to an alley and bump into a man's chest, stumbling past him, ignoring his curse. Two blocks. One block. Then I am taking the stairs, knocking over the ceramic frog that Madd brought back from Tijuana, grabbing the key and turning it in the lock.

Home. It will never be home without her. Even now, with her scent in the air, the sheets twisted from an early morning fuck, it feels wrong. I shut the door, not wanting to let out any of her air, and move to the counter, grabbing her keys, phone, and wallet. I am torn between wanting to examine every item, to grab her sweater and inhale her scent, and the urgency that pushes me forward. She may be alive. She may die. I need to get to the hospital. I grab a trash bag from underneath the sink and stuff into it the first two stacks of folded clothes from the top of the dryer. Folded by her. I shove my feet into flip-flops and run downstairs, pocketing the key, yanking the door shut behind me.

The hospital. I've broken at least nine laws to get here. I leave the truck under a red sign that flashes 'ER' and grab her things, run into the lobby, and approach the desk.

She is alive. It is the first thing I ask and is answered without hesitation, followed instantly by two words that make my heart drop and chest ache. "For now." I can't take this roller coaster. The high that I hear at the announcement of her breath, intense joy flooding my veins. Despair at the possibility that I might still lose her. They won't let me back there. Not yet. Not until some future point that is not explained by the haggard receptionists. Then the door opens, and a woman in white steps out, her eyes finding me and stepping forward.

"Are you the boyfriend?"

"Yes."

She smiles, the motion not reaching her eyes. "She is breathing, but it is assisted. She's had pretty severe head trauma. That, combined with the six or seven minutes she was without air ... we have induced a coma until we can get her stabilized."

"Induced a coma? So she can be brought out of it?"

She looks into my eyes. "If she still has brain function. She may not make it to a point where it is feasible to pull her out of it. You should call her family, any close friends, and have them come here. She may not survive the night."

I ignore the sentence, even as it stands in the center of my mind and shouts, overpowering any thought process I struggle to have. "Can I see her?"

She glances at her watch. "They're working on her now. I'll have someone come out in about thirty minutes." She smiles grimly and turns, her coat flaring out, and she is gone, the white doors swinging shut behind her.

They're working on her now.
You should call any family or friends.

I step forward dumbly, until I am before a chair, and I turn, sinking into it, my hand loosening around her wallet and phone, the items sliding into my lap. Call family or friends.

Friends. Madd doesn't really have a lot of friends. We have a big group who we hang out with—several of the guys professionally surf, and all of the girls hang out together. But they are the type you call when you are five blocks away and have a flat tire. Not when you are on life support and might not last the night. Madd and I could disappear from this stretch of beach, and it'd be weeks before anyone noticed.

Family. Madd's entire family consists of one drunken individual. A mother who I vaguely remember being in Tuscany. But I'll call her cell, just to make sure. I open her phone and scroll down the numbers, looking for 'M.' Just one contact line up from it, my breath stops.

LOVER.

Him. If I love half of her heart with my whole one, this man has claim to the other half. The other half of that heart that is struggling to beat. I have seen his name displayed on her phone before. But never have I had the desire to call. I have no need to disrupt the perfection that is our life, no need to rock that boat. I know nothing about this man. He may be married. Older. Younger. Black. White. He is wealthy; I know that. Her wrist and ears often glittering with presents, the new convertible in our garage proof of that. I know he wanted her to have a steady man, is regretful of his time spent away from her. That is either because he doesn't care, because she is a piece of ass who he uses when he can—or because he loves her and wants what's best for her. And knows she would not put up with being put in the corner. Played with when he has time and otherwise ignored. There is so much I don't know about this man. So much I never wanted to find out. But here I am, her phone in my hand, his name staring at me.

I am torn. She never wants us to meet. Wants our lives to play out separately. And I am torn between respecting those wishes and knowing what I, if I were him, would want. To hold her warm hand in mine in case it went cold forever. To hear her soft breath before it stopped eternally. If she wakes, she may hate me for it. But if she doesn't, I might not forgive myself for taking this moment from him.

PAUL

I press the CALL button, working through words in my head, steeling myself for an unknown outcome. How will I react to hearing his voice? Will he be friendly? Cold? Will I leave a message if the machine comes on? The female voice surprises me, chirping through the receiver with friendly efficiency. "Hey Madison."

I look at the phone, at the word, LOVER, clearly displayed on the front. I have dialed the right number.

"Madison?"

I clear my throat. "I was trying to reach ..." I feel sluggish, like my brain can't formulate a single articulate sentence.

"Stewart? You were calling for Stewart?" the perky voice asks helpfully.

Stewart. That is his name. A name that inappropriately brings to mind visions of my brother's face. A brother I haven't thought of in some time. I swallow, returning to the uncomfortable task at hand. "Yes. Is he available?"

"Mr. Brand is in a meeting right now. Does Madison need me to interrupt him?" Her tone is distractingly cheerful, so much so that my brain takes a moment to catch up, to focus on the insanity that just left her lips.

"Mr. Brand?" My words come out unintentionally harsh. "Stewart *Brand*?"

"Yes. Is there a problem?"

My head comes up with a jerk, and my eyes open wide, moving wildly, trying to sort out the disaster unfolding before me. I hear her voice, in my ear, the words twisting around into unintelligible forms. I close the phone, spots appearing before my eyes, and I try to breathe, try to focus on what is before me and what is important. Madd. Lying a few walls away. Dying.

But my brain won't release itself, won't step away from the bomb that was just dropped in my lap. Stewart. My older brother. *Fucking* Madd. Touching her skin, holding her body, kissing her mouth. My brother. *He* is the one who has the other half of her heart. He is the one who I share her with. He is the one who dictated a second boyfriend. He is the one too busy to fully occupy her bed, her time.

Stewart.

My brother.

The one who beat up Noah Richardson when I was eleven because Noah wouldn't stop bullying me. The one who coached me through asking Nicki Farrahs out when I was too chicken. The one who explained sex and going down on a girl and who bought me my first box of condoms. The one who punched me in the face and blames me for causing our little sister's death. The one who told me never to step within a mile of him ever again. The one who wouldn't return my calls for five years, until I finally gave up and stepped away from the tattered remains of our family.

Stewart is Him. Stewart is LOVER.

The phone rings in my hand, and I see his moniker pop up on the screen. Before I can second-guess the action, I walk over and hand it to the ER receptionist. "Please explain to them about Madison Decater," I request softly.

The woman shoots me a questioning look and then glances at the phone and flips it open. "Venice Regional ER," she says with efficiency into the phone.

I walk back to the chair and watch her face, watch her lips as they mouth words I can only guess. Wonder who is on the other end. If it is Stewart or the cheerful female. And wonder what I will do when he walks through these doors. And if she will still be alive when he does.

STEWART

We are in the middle of a deposition, when there is a knock on the door, and Ashley steps in. I look up in warning, one that softens instantly when I see her face. I hold up a finger, pausing our attorney, the transcriber looking up in surprise when the room falls silent.

She moves quickly to my side and leans forward, her lips close to my ear. "It's Madison. There's been an accident."

I close my eyes, unprepared for the words. Not again. Not after Jennifer. I slide back my chair, standing, and meet the attorney's eyes. "I have personal business to attend to. We will need to reschedule."

"Personal business?" the man stammers. "Stewart, it took a month to coordinate this."

I ignore him, following Ashley out of the room, my hand on her back, pulling her into my office and shutting the door. "Tell me. Everything."

My assistant, a current of cheer who hides a spine of steel, is shaken. It is a look I have never seen on her, her inner strength often putting my ass in place when needed. But now, she quakes before me, and the tremble in her voice weakens my core. "A man called from her phone. He wanted you, but hung up when I told him you were busy. It seemed odd ... so I called back to get his name, a message, something. A woman answered, someone from the hospital. She said that Madison was in a surfing accident and is on life support. That she might not make it through the night. That any close family and friends should come now." Tears well in her eyes, and she steps forward, reaching for my arm. "I'm so sorry, Stewart."

I brush off her touch. "Where is my phone?"

She thrusts it out, and I grab it, trying to walk through a logical thought process, my mind heavy with thoughts. "Have a driver meet me out front."

"Done. I called them before I stepped in. They have the hospital address, and I have given the hospital your information."

I nod. "Also give them my card information. Any medical expenses charge to me. I don't want any treatment or options unexplored due to cost. Make sure they understand that."

She nods quickly, tears leaking from the corner of her eyes. She knows Madison well, has lunched with her countless times, chats with her in the reception area when my meetings run over. Picked out her birthday, anniversary, and Valentine's Day gifts for the last two and a half years. I nod to her and open the door.

We make the half-hour drive in fifteen minutes, my frustration at not having my car disappearing as soon as the driver makes the first hairpin turn at forty-five miles per hour. I cradle my head in my hands, visions of Madison assaulting me from all directions.

Her head on my pillow, a drugged smile on her lips when I kiss her goodbye in the morning.
The image of her in my t-shirt, walking barefoot through my hall, nothing underneath but skin.
The push of her hands on my chest, small but firm, her ability to weaken my resolve with one saucy smile.

I should have set aside my work, should have cancelled meetings, planned vacations, made half the money and had twice the time with her. I should have taken her to dinner each night, been there for each birthday and holiday, met her mother, kissed her over breakfast, told her more of how I felt. If she is gone … if I don't have a chance to say goodbye … she will never know how I really feel. How I cherish her.

I'm an idiot.

The car pulls up to glass doors, and I open the door, steeling myself for the possibilities that await me.

She will be okay. She will live. I can make changes to my life and make her mine. Marry her. Rebuild my life the way it should be, with her front and center.

I step out of the car and move toward the glass doors of the hospital.

PAUL

Inhale.

Exhale.

Inhale.

Exhale.

I hear her breaths and hope that she is making them, hope that if this machine was to be turned off, that the controlled sounds of life would continue. I listen to the beep of her heart rate and watch the numbers on the screen, numbers that mean nothing to me.

I touch her hand softly, running my fingers over the top of it—its cool surface scaring the hell out of me. I hold it in my hands, the fingers limp and unresponsive.

"There is brain activity." The words come from behind me, and I turn to see a young male nurse, outfitted in green scrubs. He smiles. "Something came across the monitors a few minutes ago. It's a good sign."

"So she'll be okay?"

His grin falters. "No. I didn't mean that. But with her condition … we didn't expect any brain activity. We are still a long way from stability."

I nod and turn back to her. Squeeze her hand. There is nothing more heartbreaking than a limp hand. No life. No response. I lean over and place a soft kiss on a bit of exposed skin on her cheek—tubes and masks preventing any real connection.

I hear a commotion, raised voices, and the squeak of shoes on floor, and I know, without turning, Stewart is here. My hand tightens, without thought, on hers.

OVER THE FALLS: [PHRASE]
**GETTING PITCHED HEADFIRST AND
SLAMMED BY THE LIP OF A CRASHING WAVE.**

STEWART

The woman before me is infuriating. She blinks at me, gray hair covering half of her brown eyes, and purses her lips. "Only close friends and immediate family may go in. She is in ICU and already has one visitor."

"I'm her boyfriend. Stewart Brand. My assistant should have called, you spoke with her earlier."

"Her *boyfriend* is already in there. So unless we have a love triangle going on, I need to speak with him first. He's the one who brought her in, he's the one who has her identification."

I grind my teeth at the title, never regretting a single decision more in my entire life than when I hear her reedy voice give ownership of Madison to another man. "I don't need to explain the dichotomy of our relationship with you. Call Security if you wish, but I will be the one paying for her care and I—despite what you have been told—am her boyfriend. Fiancé once she pulls through."

"If she pulls through." The woman's words are firm but gentle, the statement reminding me that Madison's health is more important than the cockfight I am creating in my mind.

"I'll find her room myself. Here is my card should you feel the need to get authorities involved." I flip a business card out between my fingers and set it on her desk. Then I move forward, glancing in and out of rooms, ignoring the sputter of her voice behind me. I pass a room with a man standing alongside a bed, and then stop, stepping backward, glancing at the chart hanging on the door.

Madison Decater. Room F. This is it.

I step inside quietly, pulling the door closed, the voices instantly muffled, and move forward, my eyes only on her, the man at her side stepping back, his figure muted in my peripheral vision, my horror growing as I look at the frail figure who is my heart.

She lies in a hospital bed, her face covered with a breathing mask, tubes and cords running from portable stands to her body, face, and hands. The mechanical breathing of the machine is like a beast, huffing hot breath out that sounds nothing like her sweet sighs of sleep.

"My baby," I whisper. "Oh my God, my sweet, sweet girl." Tears spill. Tears I didn't even know my body could still create. I haven't cried since Jennifer, not even at Mother's funeral. But this, seeing her before me, struggling to breathe, artificially hanging onto life ... it is as if I am seeing my life dissolve right before my eyes with no way of rescuing it. Her life, her fire ... it is gone. It is gone, and I am faced with the sudden reality that it may never come back. I am faced with my mistakes, etched in stone, unable to be wiped clean and rewritten. I sink to my knees beside her bed and hold her hand—her limp, cold hand. I pull it to my cheek, a tear leaking down, my breath gasping as I press soft kisses onto her palm.

I've known I love her. I've known that she is the light in my life and keeps my world from being too dark, too consumed with work. But I haven't known, haven't realized until now how my love for her works. How it is more than affection. How it is the only part of me that has life. She is the only feeling that exists in my body, the only feeling that isn't tied to greed or competition or ego. She is my light, and I haven't realized it until now, when it is so close to being extinguished.

I lay my head on her chest, wrapping my arms around and under her body, gently gripping her to me. "I need you, baby. I love you so much."

There is a small cough, and I remember the other man in the room. The other man in her life. A man who, at this point in time, needs to take his leave, to step out of her life and allow me to take my rightful place. I release her gently and straighten, staring at her closed eyes, and squeeze her hand before turning to face her other man.

Seeing Paul's face pulls the final nail from the coffin that is my sanity. He stands tall, taller than I remember, his chest strong, eyes fierce, blazing with the same passion I feel behind mine. I have seen his photo, Dana's letters occasionally containing a news article or magazine clipping. But a photo wasn't needed to know who he would grow into. I have memorized every line of his face since he was a child. Admired his athletic build, his skill in the water, his easy smile and infectious laugh. He was always our golden child, the one who talked his way out of trouble, rescued stray animals, and waltzed through life with an ease—just like Madison. The thought hits me hard, the similarities terrifying in their possibilities.

I freeze, examine the look in his eyes, try to pierce the possibilities together, try to understand exactly what his presence means and pray to God that it is not what it appears. "Why are you here?"

"For the same reason you are." He nods toward the bed, toward the woman who I've spent the last two years thinking of as my own. I knew there was another man. Hell, I'm the reason she settled down with one. I didn't want her fucking half the town, going home with strangers. I wanted to know she had a steady relationship, had someone to go home to, someone to watch out for her and care for her in my absence. I just never thought of that person having thoughts and feelings for her, having ownership of her. I've always pushed that reality to the side, work taking center stage, everything else flowing, the well-oiled machine not one I needed to examine too closely. Realizing that he is her other man ... Paul falls in love with baby kittens. I don't have to look in his eyes to know he is head over heels for her. Jesus Christ, I've fucked to the thought of her with him!

My legs have lost all strength, my knees physically threatening to buckle. I stagger a few steps to the side, collapsing into the closest chair and close my eyes. There is a vibration in my pocket—my phone—and I reach in and hold the button on the side, depressing it until it vibrates and is off. "How long?" The words come out a whisper, and I clear my throat.

"The doctor should be back in about an hour with some results. We will know more then." I crack open my eyes to see him sit in a chair opposite me, leaning forward, his elbows on his knees, his eyes looking at her, and then at me.

"No." My voice is stronger, though it still cracks as I speak. "*How long* have you been fucking her?" I open my eyes and look into his.

PAUL

My brother has changed so much. At twenty years old he was already serious, dedicated to school when I was partying, his brow furrowed over grades and projections, current events, and our family's finances. Worry. Worry. Worry. At a point in his life when he should have been partying and fucking. Enjoying life. But he is even worse now. He has fully evolved into a rock hard frame of intensity. When he opens his eyes and stares at me, it is like being in the path of a train, frozen to the spot, unable to move even though the ground is trembling underfoot.

"A year and a half ... almost two. We met in Santa Monica."

"So this ... this is coincidence?" His voice is hard, unbelieving, and it is through his petulant tone that I fully believe it is solely happenstance.

I had worked through the scenario before he arrived, turning over the realization of his identity in my head, trying to figure out the pieces, and what my part is in this twisted game. There are three possibilities. One: He sent Madd to me— some fucked up situation that reeked of anything but the levelheaded Stewart I knew. Two: Madd sought out two brothers, for reasons known only to her, a deceitful game that would only end in disaster. Also completely opposite of the woman I love. Three: It was all a coincidence. A fucked up, someone-upstairs-is-screwing-with-you, coincidence.

"It's either coincidence, or she somehow orchestrated this situation." I glance toward her bed. "And I don't think she would do that."

He closes his eyes, drops his head back against the wall. "No. She wouldn't. Plus, I'm the one who pushed her to take a boyfriend."

"Why?" It is a question I have always wondered. Why a man would send someone like Madison out into the world, not concerned with the possibility of losing her. It is a question I have always contained, not wanting to rock the boat with Madd and a little scared at what the answer might be.

He sighs, opening his eyes to stare at the ceiling. "I assume you know how she is, with sex. From the beginning, I couldn't give her the time she needed. For sex, for a relationship. She deserved a full-time boyfriend, and she knew it. Refused to be exclusive with me. And I couldn't stop thinking about her. I wanted her as a constant in my life, but I wanted her to be safe, and happy, and loved. And ... fuck. Satisfied. I didn't want her out fucking around. And I didn't want her out of my life." He pushes away from the wall with his shoulder and meets my gaze. "I thought if she had a man, someone to spend her days and nights with—someone who understood that I was there, that I had a place in her life—it would keep her happy and give me a spot in her life. Give our relationship some security."

I frown. "Without you ... I could have had a normal relationship with her. *I* could have made her happy." My voice strengthens as I speak, anger coursing through my veins. "I could have been everything she needed."

He laughs, a short bark that only pisses me off more. "Paul, you're a kid. You float through life in some imaginary world, in which you do what you love and are lucky enough, so far, to make enough to live off. What are you going to do when you can't surf anymore? How are you going to provide for her? At some point in time you have to join the real world. And the real world changes people. The real world takes your cheery little smile and turns you in a dark cloud of reality. It drowns you in bills and expectations and adds piece after piece of reality onto your shoulders until you are struggling under the weight of it all." He stares at me, his features tight, face angry, and I want nothing more than to punch him, hard enough to crush bones and draw blood, but his words stop me. Words filled with as much anger as conviction. "You *can't* be everything she needs. You are a fuck. Probably a good one. And you are fun. You've done a good job of keeping her company. But you can't be her everything. You are barely your own everything. And you will fail her. Just like you failed Jennifer. Fuck—you were probably with her when this happened. Were you?" He stands, stepping closer to me, his eyes dark, his jaw tight. "Were you *there* when she drowned? Did you just let her die, like you did with Jennifer? How many women who I love are you going to hurt with that smile? With that casual attitude that lets everything important slip through the cracks?"

There is a level when your heart breaks past the point of repair. When it shatters into pieces that cannot be glued back together. His words are knives into my chest, the truth behind them lacing the blades with poison. At some point in his speech I stand, my temper flashing as I face his affront. But—halfway through his final words, when the truth and guilt burn into my soul, I weaken—in the end, I drop to my knees, my hands falling to my side, my eyes wincing when the final stone finds its mark and shakes my soul.

I barely notice when he steps away, when he moves out the door, and the click of the door sounds.

Inhale.
Exhale.
Inhale. Exhale.

Her haggard breathing is the only sound in the room until I sob, gripping the bars of the gurney, holding onto them tightly and leaning against her bed. "Please wake up," I plead to her unresponsive body. "Please, baby. Please. I love you and need you so much."

I do. I need her arms around me. Her eyes, staring, smiling into mine. They make me feel as if I can do no wrong. As if all we have is time and our time is golden. No worries, no regrets. Two people running through life with our arms outstretched and the sun on our back. We don't need much. We have love. We will make everything else work. Fuck Stewart. Fuck him and his speech and his intensity.

I love her.
I need her.
I need her.
I need her.

I sob and pray reverently—pray for forgiveness and for her.

Madison. My heart.

STEWART

I cannot go back in there. I cannot go back after the words I just said. I cannot face him after I saw his face crumble. He has stood up to me so rarely in his life. And in there, in his anger and his accusation ... I saw the man he has become. The man he has grown into. He was right. Without me and my selfish need to have her light, he could have had a normal relationship. Whether it had been him, or someone else, she would have found a normal life. Someone one hundred percent devoted to her rather than a job. Someone whose entire focus was making her happy. Someone who fucked her senseless so she didn't need a second cock. His words were honest and hit home, and I pushed back with every pissed off bone in my body.

I stripped him bare and left him there. Alone with his insecurities.

I can't go back in there. But she's in there, and so I have to go back. I can't leave her alone. But I can't face him again.

I am an asshole.

He is my brother.

She has my heart.

Fuck.

DANA

I am at lunch, sipping artificially-sweetened strawberry lemonade and debating between a Caesar salad or tuna roll when my phone rings. I consider ignoring it. It is probably the office, and I don't feel like dealing with numbers and IRS regulations right now. I let it ring three times before my OCD gets the best of me, and I slide my finger across the screen without looking at it, lifting it to my ear and catching the eye of the waiter. "Hello?"

"Dana. It's me." The catch in his voice has me instantly alert, my hand waving the approaching waiter away with a hurried motion.

"What's wrong? Is it Paul?" I feel a tightness in my chest I haven't feel in ten years, not since I stood in front of my mother and heard the news that broke apart our world.

"No. Yes." He breathes deeply, and I suddenly see him, my brother, pinching the bridge between his eyes, inhaling as he struggles with whatever it is that is about to come out of his mouth. "Paul is fine. But I need you. Can you come to Venice Regional?"

"The hospital?" I am on my feet and moving, my purse in my hand, abandoning my drink, my hip hitting the corner of a table hard. I wince; that's gonna leave a bruise.

"Yes. How soon can you be there?"

"Fifteen minutes. I—I moved back to L.A. A year ago." I feel guilty saying the words. But its not like he's answered any of my calls. Hard to share information with a brick wall.

"I'll be in the ER lobby. Please hurry."

The phone goes dead in my hand, and I jog to my car, my heels clipping on the sidewalk, my hand stuffing the phone into my purse. I feel momentary disappointment that he didn't comment on my move—we are, after all, in the same city now. But I knew that wouldn't matter much to him. It wasn't as if he had the time, or desire, to meet for lunch or grab dinner one night. It didn't matter to him if I was fifteen minutes or fifteen hours away. But he needs me now. And that makes my heart beam. He needs someone, and he called me. Paul is fine. Whatever is wrong, both of my boys are safe. I unlock my car.

I see him as soon as I step inside the lobby, his tall frame tense, his legs moving quickly to me, and he grabs me tightly, wrapping his arms around me, pressing a tight kiss on my head. "Let's step outside," he whispers.

He speaks to the receptionist, a gray-haired woman who regards him with disdain, an odd reaction to Stewart's looks and traditional charm.

We step into the afternoon heat, and he releases my arm, moves to the side and leans against a column of the overhang. "You got a light?"

"A cigarette?" I stare at him. I dig in my purse, pulling out a pack of Marlboros and a lighter. "What happened to your health kick?"

"It just ended." He taps one out and lights it, cupping his hand around the flame and inhaling deeply.

I take the pack from him and shake out another, stuffing the box back in my purse. "What's going on, Stewart? As delighted as I am to hear from you, it's been two years."

He blows out a stream of smoke. "I know, Dana. I'm sorry about that. You know what life's like. Time is gone … before you even know it."

"Whatever. I don't think you have any idea what life's like. You know what work's like."

He is silent for a moment, staring out at the parking lot. Then he looks over at me, his gaze intense. The intense gaze that he's had since he was eight, a stare that cuts through any bullshit that might exist, one that protects him while he invades your soul. "I don't need your depressing views of my life. I called you here because I need your help."

I bite back the sharp retort that sits hot on my tongue. "Then talk to me."

He looks out onto the street. "It's about a girl."

Reality hits me like a hundred pound wrecking ball, and I curse my own stupidity. Duh. I know only one fact about his current life. One blonde fact who prances between him and Paul. *Of course* this is about her. How did it take me five minutes to get to this bright, shiny light bulb of obviousness? I should have known it the minute I heard his voice. "Go on."

"I'm in love." I tilt my head, stepping closer to him, the foreign word surprising. "She's amazing, D. She's amazing and beautiful, and I've screwed it all up."

I keep my mouth shut, sucking on the end of the cigarette.

"I was too busy. Working—you know my schedule. She wouldn't give me an exclusive relationship, not when I could only see her once a week or so."

I arch my brow and glance over at his handsome profile, a sliver of grudging respect wedging its way into my "I hate this woman" campaign. "She shouldn't have. You don't have time for a house plant, much less a woman."

He thumbs the cigarette before placing it between his lips. "I know. So I told her to see someone else. I told her I'd share her. Told her to date him and me at the same time."

I almost say Paul's name. Almost blow my cover. I swallow the words and aim for a casual tone. "*Share* her? With who?"

He shrugged. "I didn't know. Didn't care. I just told her to find someone who made her happy. Someone who understood that I wasn't going anywhere."

"And you thought *that* would work out?" I toss my cig to the side and step on it, crossing in front of Stewart and planting my feet, staring up into eyes that I haven't seen in far too long. "You thought what? She'd date both of you? Forever?"

He meets my stare solidly. "It was that or lose her. What was I supposed to do?"

I scoff, an expression that trips and somehow becomes an unladylike snort. "Work a normal schedule. Cut back to eighty hours a week. Enjoy life. Have an actual relationship with someone. Not timeshare her out!"

His face hardens, lines forming where there once were none. "I regret it now. I know I fucked up. But at the time—I didn't love her then. I had just met her. I didn't know where it would go."

I look into his eyes. "You *love* her." I test the words on my tongue, knowing, as I stare into his eyes, that he means it. That my big, strong, only-cares-about-work brother has fallen in love. Then I remember where we are standing, and my blood runs cold. "Why are we here, Stewart? What happened?"

His face crumbles for a moment, a flash of weakness before he busies himself with a puff of smoke. "There was an accident," he says softly, the last word swelling in his mouth. "A surfing accident. They don't think she's gonna make it."

A surfing accident. This situation suddenly has taken a nosedive into hell. I don't need to ask if Paul was there. I don't need to know the many parallels must exist to tie this incident to the one ten years ago. I swallow hard, and my heart aches for my boys.

He wipes at his face, pressing both hands over it, the cigarette burning down, close to his skin, my desire to keep him from being hurt overridden by my understanding that I should give him space. "Paul," he chokes out. "Paul was who she found. God's twisted fuckaround in our lives. And when I found out ... God Dana ... the things I said to him." He drops his hands, drops the burning cigarette to the ground and falls back against the column, his eyes staring out, red and filled with tears. "How did this all happen?"

I go to him, wrapping my arms around his waist and hugging him tightly as my mind sorts through all that he has just said. I had the entire situation wrong, had never dreamed that they were willingly sharing her with an unknown stranger. "Does he love her?" I pulled back and look up at Stewart. "Paul. Does he love her, too?"

"He's Paul."

I understand instantly what he means. Paul is a lover. He loves freely and easily; his love accepts faults and is unconditional in its strength. He wouldn't be with her if he didn't love her.

"Will you go talk to him?"

"I think you should," I say gently. "I think you're about ten years overdue."

His jaw tightens. "He shouldn't have let her go with them. You know that."

I glare at him. "He was fucking nineteen! And Jennifer's not coming back, whether the relationship between you two is intact or ruined. But you know what she would have wanted." I pull at his arm—make him look me in the eye. "She would have wanted you to be close. To be what you used to be."

He meets my stare, his shoulders dropping slightly. "I can't do it, Dana. I can't go back in there after the things I said. Just go find out what he's thinking. I called you here because I need you. We need you."

I can't deny that request. Not when it is the first time one of my brothers has reached out to me in years. I give him one final hug and then step back inside, anxious to see Paul. It has been so long.

PAUL

I rest my head on her stomach, feel the rise and fall of her chest, and wonder how long they will let me stay. Wonder if it is a doctor or my brother who will make me leave. I am caught off guard when a soft female hand touches my arm. Pulls it. I close my eyes and take a final breath of Madd's scent before I rise to follow the nurse.

But it isn't a nurse. I am so confused at her face—Dana—a face I haven't seen in years. After Jennifer—after Stewart's accusations and the guilt of her death—I couldn't be around the family. Couldn't be reminded of the decision I made that killed her. And now she is here. A damn family reunion in the middle of Madd's hospital room. I feel a flash of anger at the intrusion, mixed with the confusing joy at seeing her. Dana was our glue, our strength. She held us together until the point when everything fell apart. And in this moment of breakage, I want nothing more than to wrap my arms around her. "What are you doing here, Dana?"

She walks over to Madison. Glances at the monitors. "Stewart called me. He explained … the situation."

I step backward, until I feel the edge of the chair, and sink into it. "He blames it on me. Again."

She shakes her head, turning to look at me, her profile aged since I saw her last. A few shots of gray through her hair, barely-there crow's feet around her eyes. "No, he doesn't. That's his emotions talking. Just like it was with Jennifer. He's mad at the situation. You're just the closest thing for him to take it rage out on. Brush it off."

"I don't want to brush it off. It's bullshit. Bullshit that I—and Madison—don't need."

She tilts her head at me. "You can't speak for her. You want to speak up for yourself—fine. I think you should. I think you should tell Stewart every thing that you've pent up over the last decade. I think you should tell him exactly how you feel about her, and exactly how you want this to end. He deserves you to verbally kick his ass, and he deserves to know how you feel about her. But it's a two-way street. And you need to be prepared to hear what he says, too."

"I heard what he said. He made it clear what he thinks of me."

"But do you know what he thinks of her?"

Her soft tone makes me pause, makes me consider my next words before releasing them. "No. But I saw his reaction when he saw her. It … it wasn't what I would expect, knowing Stewart as I—we—once did." I look up to see her nodding, her mouth tight. "He loves her." The words crush out of me, words that I have held back from myself, refusing to see what was so clearly laid out in devastating order before me. She moves beside me, taking the seat to my left, her hand reaching out and looping through mine, tugging it to her.

I know," she whispers.

I lean into her, smelling the scent of her perfume, different than what she used to wear. Her hair is now dark, a chocolate brown that suits her, and she is wearing a suit. I frown, looking at the dark pinstripe of her pants. I don't even know where she works—if she is still in accounting or if she has moved to a different field. I look at the bed, at the still figure there. "What do I do, Dana? This whole thing is so fucked up ..."

"You talk to him," she whispers, patting my hand. "Go out and talk to him, away from her."

I shake my head. "I'm not leaving her. Not when any moment ..." My words break. I swallow. "The doctor says she's still unstable."

She grips my arm, the hold tight. "You don't need to fight over her body. Talk outside, let her have peace to heal."

I turn, letting her see, through my eyes, my resolve. "Bring him here. She's as much a part of this as we are. I'm not stepping away from this bed 'til they drag me away. Please."

Her eyes sink a bit, and I can see disappointment in their depths, her grip weakening on my arm. "Fine." She lets go of my arm. "I'll go talk to him."

"Hey," I call out, a moment too late, as the door is swinging shut behind her. I reach for the handle, but her foot kicks back, holding the door, her eyes looking expectantly my way. "I missed you. Thanks for coming."

She steps backward, and I move forward for a hug. A tight embrace that reminds me of what I have missed out on. "I love you," she whispers.

"I love you, too."

STEWART

I walk down the hall, nurses barely glancing up, the drama of earlier gone. They have now accepted the fact that Madison has two boyfriends, and that we are both present, the additional female regarded as a non-issue. I check my messages outside, six new voicemails all urgently demanding a callback. I have not called them back, but they weigh on my mind, poking my brain at inopportune moments.

Madison has never asked me to cut back my hours. She accepted my schedule, my obligations. She just explained, in no uncertain terms, that schedule would mean non-exclusivity.

A part of me wonders if I'll be able to do it. Be able to cut back. Work less. Delegate more. Six voicemails. I shouldn't be thinking of them—not when her life hangs in the balance.

I hesitate outside the door, taking a deep breath and steeling myself. For the image of her, plugged in and supported with cords and machines. For the image of him, my baby brother, stars in his eyes and all grown up, ready to fight me over the woman I love.

I push the door open and step into the room. His head tilts up, his eyes steady on mine. He stands on the opposite side of her bed, and I step forward, until the only thing separating us is her body. His eyes are wet but steady. This is not the same man who crumbled under my words an hour earlier. This man has fight in his eyes, strength in his shoulders. And I am suddenly hit with a burst of pride in him.

I come to a stop, and we stare at each other for a long moment without speaking.

"You can't have her." His voice is strong, resolute.

I glance to the monitors. "Neither one of us might get that opportunity."

Anger lights his face. "She'll make it. You don't know her. She's strong."

I want to respond, to put him in his place, but the truth hits me hard. I *don't* know her. I know her body, every last inch of it. I can close my eyes and draw out every curve of her skin, freckle on her face, flex of her muscles. I can tell from her breathing when she is about to come, can describe the moan she makes when she needs it harder, the gasp when my length has hit the place where she likes it. But her? I have spent too little time with her. I love her, but I need more time to *know* her. I don't know what time she wakes up in the morning, don't know her favorite ice cream flavor, or what caused the small scar on the back of her knee. I don't know her mother's name, her TV shows, or how she likes her steak. But I do know that Paul is right. She has fire. She has fight. If there is a way, her mind will make it happen. I look down at her. "You love her."

"Yes. I'm not letting her go."

I pull my gaze back to him, my eyes heavy, not wanting to see what rests there. Resolve. "You fall in love easily, Paul. You don't know what—"

"You don't know me anymore, Stewart. You don't have the right to tell me how I love. I'm not the nineteen year old kid you walked out on."

No, he isn't. I feel lost, like I have no footing in this room and am questioning every word that comes out of my mouth while he—he is so secure. Strong. Like this is his room, and I am an intruder in it, instead of the other way around. "She was mine first, Paul. I had her. I told her to find someone to keep her entertained." I looked at him. "Entertained, Paul. That was it. I was always the primary in this relationship. You were the secondary."

"Your work is the primary. Everything else in your life comes secondary." His voice rises, and he points to me, then to her. "Tell me that isn't true. Tell me you didn't put her to the side while you slaved away for your job. Tell me she wasn't an afterthought to your business and deals."

I can't. I softly run a hand over hers, wanting to get on my knees and beg for forgiveness. I curse his presence for being here right now. When all I want is to be alone with her and tell her how I feel. Tell her the mistakes I've made. Apologize for any and every time that I put her second in my life. I clear my throat. "I can't fix what I've done. I can only change going forward."

"Bullshit. You aren't going to step in as a Monday-morning quarterback. I gave her my heart two years ago, spent every day of that time being there for her. This is the woman I wake up next to every day. Every day except when you snap your fingers and steal her for the night. I breathe and live for her. She is mine, despite what you think or say."

There is a soft cough behind me, and I turn, seeing Dana in the doorway, her steps moving in. She crosses her arms and shoots us both a look. "I don't hear either one of you thinking about *her*. She doesn't belong to either of you. You're both acting like you hold any decision-making rights in her life, like you can fistfight your way to a victory. Who would *she* pick, if she was awake right now?"

I look away from Dana and Paul and down at her. Look at her closed eyes and the rise and fall of her chest. And I am absolutely terrified of the answer.

DANA

I don't know what to make of my brothers. Of the men they have become. They snarl and snap over her silent body like she is the last scrap of meat, and they are starving. They are both desperate in their love, both terrified of losing her. Both reckless in their announcement of happily ever after. But they forget the most important thing: they don't have much of a choice in this. That her heart, her damaged brain, will decide if she ever wakes up. If they ever get a chance to look in her eyes and tell her how they feel. And if she does wake up, it will be her choice to make.

I, myself, am torn. Over this woman, over my feelings for her. I have spent the last two months hating her. Secretly watching, trying to figure out her motives, her plan. And now ... it appears she has no plan at all. Stewart was the executor of this insane figure eight. She is just the center of it. The place where the two halves come together and meet.

This entire situation is a disaster.

It is at this point in time that the beeping, the slow beeping that has been the heartbeat of this horror show slows, the change in tempo catching all of our attention. Lights that I never noticed begin to flash, alarms begin to sound, and all I can focus on is the beeping has stopped.

Stopped.

Flatline.

Both men rush to her body as the door slams open and white coats swarm.

MADISON

I cannot speak for others who have died. Their experiences might have been different. They might have been met at glittery gates by Morgan Freeman and cute little cherubs with cheeks of sparkles. I only know that it felt like being pulled. Not pulled forward in a vacuum of suck, but pulled apart, each arm and limb yanked slowly, an excruciating pain as cracks formed in bone, tissue, and muscles popping and ripping, my chest struggling to pump as ventricles broke loose and cavities collapsed. My heart struggled to pick a side as my body broke in half, tearing down the middle in the unclean division of all the things that made my body whole. Its pieces were stubborn, sewn into ribcages and sternums, and it finally yanked into two separate pieces, my soul screaming in protest as I was released to the heavens.

PAUL

There is shouting, unintelligible words, and we are pushed aside, the small room suddenly full, my back hitting the sharp edge of a machine. I struggle to see her face, my panicked eyes meeting Stewart's, despair in his blue eyes. Our gaze holds for a moment, and in that moment, everything is forgiven. We need only one thing ... and I return my gaze to her, to her body, which is so still, the monitor still showing a flat line, buzzing and alarms sounding throughout the room. I choke back a sob and watch the fury of activity, my hands clenching into fists. Then I drop to my knees and pray, silent fast words spilling from my mouth. I promise things I will never be able to deliver, promise to let her go, to let her be with him. I promise to lead a perfect life, to devout myself to good, anything, everything, just to have her live. I need her life. I cannot, will not, make it without her. I don't have to have her as mine, but I need her to live. This world cannot lose her. I cannot exist if she is not alive.

STEWART

Six voicemails. The fact that it crosses my mind in this moment is sickening. It is something I will never admit to anyone. I push it out of my mind at the moment it creeps in, desperate to bury it with emotions, love, grief, anything. I don't deserve her. I don't deserve anything but my empty office, stacked with deadlines and trades, dotted lines and stock prices. I don't deserve the sunny smile flirting with me while snow dots her face, her giggle when I awaken her at four AM, her hand tugging me to my feet while she drops to her knees. I try to catch sight of her, try to see past the flash of metal, white cloth, and gloves. I try to see her face. I try to send her a silent apology for every piece of the man that I am not. I step backward, against the wall, and pray.

DANA

There are too many people in the room, all with a purpose or a deep-ingrained love that will not allow their feet to move. I am the only one with no place in that room. I am the outsider, watching the train wreck with a morbid fascination. I can't help them. This is something they have to figure out amongst themselves. I don't envy Madison when she wakes up. An event that should be a celebration, the survival of death will be a tense, who-will-you-choose tug of war. She will wake to expectant eyes, competing affections, and pregnant pauses. I need to protect her. I need to keep their competition at bay and allow her to heal. I am suddenly struck with the irony of those thoughts. For months I have been worried about protecting them from her. And now, now that I am actually present and a part of this discussion, I have crawled over the fence and am now guarding the opposite side.

As the flatline stretches out, her body jerking with electricity from the paddles, no change, no life coming back into her body, I realize that I may not have a fence to protect. And I join my brothers in fervent prayer.

MADISON

I am brought back to life at 4:08 PM. It is with a jarring impact, my back slamming against the bed with a hard thunk. My eyes flip open to bright white light, shining intensely down on me, heads breaking the line of white, hands everywhere, touching, lifting, squeezing my skin. I briefly hear Paul's voice, and then my eyes close, and I sink back into darkness.

I am so. so. tired.

I feel a squeeze then a release. A squeeze and then a release. A hum of sounds, a familiar cadence that my brain recognizes as speech—the words unintelligible. I struggle, the grip on my hand tightening as I try to move. I open my eyes, crust sticking my lashes together, a haze over my vision, and I blink to clear them.

An unfamiliar face peers into mine—the man's features studied, his eyes sharp, looking carefully into mine. I frown, trying to place him, trying to place the white tile ceiling behind his head. Where am I? There is a roar in my head, spots appearing in my vision, and I wince, closing my eyes briefly, the peace instantly returning, and I relax against the pillow, grateful for the reprieve.

The hand squeezes again, and the voices return, incessant and irritating. I try to pull my hand away, try to roll to my side and block out the voices. I want to sleep, and this party of irritating is putting a cramp in that style.

It won't stop, and now a second hand has joined the party, squeezing my other hand. I groan, opening my eyes again, the white glare doing the tango in stilettos on my head, shooting needles straight into my temples. I try and focus, try to move my mouth and tell these persistent assholes to go to hell. I can't move my head, can't do anything but stare up into the light, and I wonder where the stranger went, if he is still here, if he is one of the damn individuals squeezing my hands to death. A new face enters my vision, and I relax slightly. Paul.

He leans forward, speaking so loudly that someone two blocks away could hear, the angle of his approach revealing that he is one of the hand squeezers. "Madd, can you hear me?"

I blink at him and try to speak. Swallow and try again, the words coming out as a whisper. "I'm not deaf. Please ... shut up and let me sleep."

He grins. The damn man grins, a smile that stretches across his face as if he has just won the Mavericks Invitational. "Yes, baby," he whispers, and I would swear that a tear leaks from his eyes.

"Thank you," I grumble, my voice coming out hoarse, my eyes closing against the still-brutal light. "And please have someone turn that damn light off."

"Anything else, babe?" His voice is close to my ear but at a normal decibel level, and I can feel the warm tickle of breath against my eardrum.

"Yeah." I sigh, the glare against the darks of my eyelids gone, some angel having found the fry light, turning it off. "Stop strangling my hands."

If he responds, I don't hear it. Darkness is once again my new best friend.

DANA

I find Stewart in one of the lobby chairs; he looks up at my approach. "Hey sis," he says dully.

"She's asleep but stable. You didn't want to stay in the room?"

He shakes his head, lifting a hand and massaging his temples.

I sit next to him, run my hand over his shoulder, picking a bit of lint off the material. "It's okay, that she didn't see you when she woke up. She'll know you were here. Chances are she won't even remember it."

He shakes his head. "It doesn't matter. The point wasn't for her to see me. I'm just glad I saw it." He lets out a breath of air. "God, when her eyes opened ... when I heard her voice ... it was a weight off my shoulders. I've never been so scared, Dana. I mean, with Jennifer, there was never an unknown period. We were just told what happened. And had to deal with it in any way we could. With Madison ... the unknown, the waiting ..." He turns his head, looking at me. "I was terrified."

I look into his eyes. Eyes that have matured so much in the last few years. His shoulders sag, as if there is no strength in his bones, his body drained of any energy or hope. And in his eyes ... I see disappointment, an emotion I don't understand. "You should go in there. She might wake back up."

His eyes darken. "No. I want Paul ... God, I don't know." He looks down, leans forward in his chair and rests his forearms on his knees. "I don't think ..." he says carefully, every word measured, "that I deserve her."

"In what way?"

He runs his fingers over his mouth. "I don't think I can do it, D." He looks back at me. "And I wouldn't tell another soul but you this. The work—the job—I don't know that I can walk from it. Cut back my hours to a level she would expect. Deserve." He snorts, disgust in his eyes. "Fuck, I can't even sit in a hospital room while she struggles for life and not think about it." He looks away. "Paul ... he doesn't struggle with that. She—in there—is all he's thinking about. All that he loves in life is her." His shoulders sink. "Do I have the right to take that from him? Only to fail her later?"

He runs a hand through his hair, gripping it before dropping his head into his hands. "But where does that leave me? A life alone? With nothing but my work? She ... she is the only thing I have other than that."

I reach out a hand and grab his knee, squeezing it hard until he looks at me, a haunted look in his eyes. "Stewart, I know that stepping away from her seems difficult. But if she was truly the girl for you – you'd happily set aside work. You wouldn't *have* to try and cut back your hours. You wouldn't be able to stay away from her. When that time comes, *that* is when you'll know that you have found the person you are meant to be with. When your life is no longer your own, and you are pushing forward that sacrifice willingly."

He holds my gaze for a long moment before glancing towards the ICU doors. "So what, you think that is how Paul feels? You think she 'is it' for him?"

I follow his glance, flipping back through everything I have seen today. "I don't know," I say carefully. "I think you and I both still see Paul as he once was—emotional and tender-hearted. But he is ten years older now. I do know that he is not the boy we once knew. And the *only* thing on his mind in there is her. He … he's not like anything I would've expected. It terrifies me how singularly focused he is on her. It's as if he thinks he can will and love her back to health."

He groans. "God, you make me feel like shit, D."

I lean against his shoulder, looping my arm through his. "You're sacrificing a piece of your life for him. This is the proudest I've ever been of you." I turn my head, my peripheral vision seeing the edge of his lips curl slightly.

"I haven't made a decision, Dana."

"Yes, you have," I say firmly. "Now go outside and make your calls. I'll tell Paul." I stand, brushing off my pants and reach for my purse, his hands stopping me, the insistent press of them causing me to pause.

"I love her." The raw need in his eyes gives me pause, a spike of pain hitting my heart.

"I know," I say softly. "But you love him, too. And you know that I'm right."

His jaw tightens.

MADISON

Kisses. Soft kisses on my cheeks, nose, moving down my neck. I shift slightly, bending my head to the face in my neck, slowly opening my eyes to—thank God—a softly lit room. The kisses find their way to my lips, and I smile, recognizing the scruff, the soft way he cradles my head. "Hey baby."

"Hey." He kisses my forehead. "How do you feel?"

"Okay." My head aches. "What time is it?"

"Almost ten. In about ten minutes their most intimidating nurse is going to come in and try and kick me out. Just in case she succeeds, I wanted to say hi."

"Hi," I say weakly, and Paul smiles.

"What happened?" I glance around the room, realizing that my neck now moves, that I can turn my head with ease. *Ouch.* After *that* blinding slice of pain, maybe I should take it easy.

"You wiped out. The board must have hit you on the head."

"I'm in the hospital for that?"

His face tightens. "You were without oxygen for a while. And with head trauma ... for a while we didn't think you'd make it."

"We?"

His eyes hold mine. "The doctors ... and also Stewart. He was here."

My heart sinks in my chest. "Here?" *With you?* The unspoken words scream through my mind.

"Yeah." He clears his throat. "But don't worry about that now. You need to rest."

"He's not here now."

"No. He left a few hours ago. Once your condition stabilized."

"And how long will you stay?"

He watches my eyes carefully. "Until they drag me away."

I smile, my eyes closing as another burst of pain lights every receptor in my brain. "My head hurts," I mumble.

I hear him stand, his hand brushing my hair back, placing a soft kiss on my forehead. "I'll get the nurse," he whispers.

I keep my eyes closed and wait for the pain to ease, my racing thoughts interfering with the process. Stewart was here. With Paul. In the same room. Speaking. Interacting. I am almost grateful for my unconscious state. I cannot imagine the words spoken, the conversations had. I would wonder at his absence—wonder what that means to our relationship, but it is Stewart. His work, no doubt, needed attention. I am surprised he stayed until I gained consciousness. I wonder what will happen with my relationships. This is surely the moment. I always thought that when this happened, I would have to choose. Which of my men I love the most. But now, with hours of unknown events, chances are, that choice has been taken from me. And in that light, Stewart's absence seems more notable.

I hear the door and reopen my eyes, watch as a nurse scurries in, pressing buttons and making adjustments. "You're awake!" she says with a beam. She lifts a remote, presses it into my palm. "This is painkiller. Just press this button if the discomfort gets too strong. I'm adding a bit into your IV, so I wouldn't be surprised if you fall back asleep pretty soon."

I nod, and place the remote on my stomach, my eyes finding Paul's. He gives me a worried smile and turns to the nurse. "How do her vitals look?"

"Good. We're not out of danger yet, but we are moving in the right direction. We'll monitor her closely tonight." She pats my arm, and I attempt a smile, the pain already less, my mind taking advantage of the increased capacity and envisioning all of the disasters that could have occurred during my sleep.

"How long was I out?" It hurts to talk, my throat raw, my lungs moaning over the expelled air.

She glances at her watch. "About twelve hours. This is the first time you've been coherent enough to talk." That's a good sign."

Twelve hours. Cities burn to the ground in less time than that. I wait for her to leave and watch Paul sit carefully on the edge of my bed. When the door clicks behind her I wet my lips.

"What happened? With Stewart?" I fight the question, hating the words as they leave my mouth. But I need to know. I need to know what tomorrow will bring. Sleep will come soon enough and wash over the reality.

"He had work to do." He glances at my face. "He'll probably be back tomorrow."

I can see his pain through his eyes, and it strikes me suddenly that I've never seen him this way. Worried. He reaches for my hand and squeezes it. I have never felt more helpless. I want to hold him, to push that darkness from his eyes. I want to go to Stewart, to make him look me in my eyes and ask him what he is thinking, where his mind is taking him. But I would probably be disappointed in the answer. His mind has probably already left this problem and is attacking ones that are in his control. In the office, on the phone, on his computer at home. I lean back and close my eyes.

I wake once to voices, arguing softly, and open my eyes enough to see a nurse, speaking heatedly to Paul. The second time I awaken, the room is dark. I turn my head and see Paul, in a chair, his head to the side. I let my eyes adjust to the room, the pain present enough for me to reach for the remote, press the button on its front.

I am grateful for the silence. For the ability to think without being observed.

I have lived in this fairytale for so long, it is hard to imagine an alternative. But this feels like the time. The time to pick a path, abandon the other and move forward. I look at the man asleep next to me, the room's shadows highlighting the strong features, his large frame uncomfortably sprawled over the hospital's narrow recliner. It is no surprise that he is here, that he won the battle against the nurse and sleeps beside me. Paul has always been here for me. He is my rock and loves me unconditionally, no matter what kind of crazy quasi-relationship we have had for the last two years.

I glance up at the ceiling, letting out a painful breath, and think of Stewart. Also, not a surprise that he is absent. Our entire relationship has been squeezed in between stretches of absence. His passion for work is one of the things I love about him, but it has always been a competing piece—the fourth person in this triangle. And I've always known where I stood in that order—behind that passion, peering over its shoulder and waving my hands for attention.

At this point, this juncture, the decision should be easy. Paul is right here, just waiting for a shot at my entire heart. He has been waiting for it ever since that day under the pier. I was just too distracted by Stewart, emotionally tied to him, to see Paul in the role he should have been in.

I reach out for him, then clear my throat, coughing slightly, and Paul instantly moves, waking, his hand swinging out and hitting a lamp. He shoots to his feet and stands still, his body tense, listening in the darkness. I softly say his name, and he steps forward, gently reaching out until his hands find my body. "Are you okay, Madd? Do you need the nurse?"

"I'm fine," I whisper. "I just ... Paul—I just wanted to say that I love you."

He stills, his breath stopping in the quiet room. "I love you, too, baby," he says gruffly, kneeling beside my bed and holding my hand. "God, I love you so much."

"Forever and always," I whisper.

He surprises me by crawling into the bed, the narrow width barely accommodating us both. He moves cords and lines with heartbreaking tenderness, turning me on my side and wrapping his arm around me. I relax, my lids heavy. At this moment in time, there is not a more perfect place I could imagine. Not another man on Earth who I want holding me.

"Forever and always," Paul whispers.

And, in that brief moment, I feel guilt over Stewart and my heart's abandonment of him. Then, pure happiness washes over me, and Stewart is forgotten.

DANA

I wake two hours early, rolling out of bed with a purpose. It is the first day in almost a decade that I have my boys back. Thanks, in no small part, to Madison. The same Madison who I, in a brief moment of creativity, dart-boarded last week after too many margaritas. But that was before. Before she almost died, and Stewart called me, and I got to hug Paul and look into both of their eyes. Before I found out that she wasn't running their hearts through a shredder for her personal enjoyment. I almost, just a teeny bit, feel some affection for the woman.

I dress for work, pulling on a Jones New York suit and sling-backs, pull my hair into a low bun and leave my contacts in their case, sticking with glasses and minimal makeup, and jog out the door at 5:45 AM, two bananas and an apple in my purse, a giant mug of coffee in my hand.

Sixteen minutes later, I step through the hospital doors, and smile brightly at the receptionist. Three minutes later, I am escorted to her room.

"She will still be asleep," the silver-haired woman explained in a hushed voice that was practically screaming. "But you can sit in there until she wakes up. Her notes say she was coherent and speaking late last night."

Late last night. After Stewart left, his phone already to his ear. She must have woken after I left at nine. Hopefully Paul was here. By the look on his face, he had had no intentions of going anywhere. I gently press on the door and tiptoe inside.

My heart swoons when I see them. A tall frame hugging her small body, crammed in a narrow space that should be uncomfortable but looks perfect. His head nestled in her hair, his arm across her body. Her eyes closed, a small smile on her face, her feet tucked back between his legs. I hesitate in the doorway, then step backward, pulling the door gently closed.

I make my way back to the receptionist area and veer right, following the path to the cafeteria, pulling my cell from my pocket as I walk. I dial Stewart's cell.

"Hey."

"Hey. I'm at the hospital. Just wanted to check and see if you were coming by."

He sighs, heavy into the phone. "I can't now. I have ..." There is the rustle of papers, and I hear him speaking to someone else. Then he is back. "Is she stable?"

"Yes." I can't stop the smile from entering my voice. "She was speaking last night. Coherent. They haven't woken her yet this morning."

He exhales loudly and all background noise stops for a moment. "That is so great, Dana. That ... God, I can't describe how that makes me feel. Have you told Paul?"

"He stayed the night." I wait to see his reaction before I say anything more, the silence long before he finally speaks.

"That's good. I'm glad someone was there when she woke up. Do you know … if she asked for me?"

"I don't know. But today … she needs to know the connection between you two. She won't understand otherwise."

His voice is suddenly abrupt. "I know. Just … handle it. However you think best. Let her know … if she asks … that I love her."

"You love her." I wait a moment. "That's it?"

"That's all I can do," he says quietly. "She'll understand. It's one of the things I love about her."

He hangs up the phone, his voice echoing in my head. *I love her. One of the things I love about her.* The silly grin, one I'd been wearing since I walked in and saw Paul cuddling with her, drops.

I sit in an uneven chair and eat rubbery eggs, staring at today's paper and trying to think. I woke up delusional, thinking that this would all turn out easy. I had thought, after talking to Stewart yesterday, that he understood. That he would walk away without looking back. Leave Paul to his happiness. Move on. I didn't factor in the fact that he still loves her. That love doesn't have an off switch. God, I knew that better than anyone. I still pine for my ex-husband, who happily lives his new life with his new wife. I go to bed each night wanting that impossibility. Who was I to think that he could, with one simple decision, step away and wash his hands of any emotion?

I take a sip of coffee and watch the clock tick, dreading the morning and all that it brings. I need to get to work. It is tax time, a deadline approaching that cannot be missed. But I don't know my younger brother well enough to trust that he will handle this correctly. Hell, *I* don't even know how to handle it correctly.

It is one giant ball of screwed up. Paul is ecstatic at the fact that she's alive. At the fact that he might have her all to himself. Stewart is brooding in his office of solitude, still tossing out emotions like shedding skin, the fresh new skin just as love-affected as what is falling off. I am being greedy, like an underfed vulture, swooping down, excited about the carnage and what it could mean for me. My two boys. Back in my life. Egos pushed aside in a time of need. And the woman who it all centers around—she is the biggest unknown. How she feels. Who she wants. Stewart has stepped away ... but what if she chases him? What is she chooses him? Paul ... I can't imagine what that would do to him.

I push back from the table and carry my tray to the trash, accidently dumping my fork in, watching as it slides down into a mountain of yuck. I debate reaching for it, then glance around casually. No one is looking. I stack the tray on top and heft my purse over my shoulder, heading back to her room.

I turn a corner and run into Paul, his hair messy, a white v-neck pulled sloppily over board shorts. His hands coming out, an apology tumbling from his mouth, and then a smile breaks over his face when he sees it's me. God, I've missed his smile. I've missed that dimple in his cheek, his carefree eyes, the sparkle in them when he is happy.

"Hey sis." He wraps his arms around me, squashing my purse to my chest in one tight embrace. "Did you hear? She's awake." He releases me, stepping back. "She's back—just like before. No damage."

I smile at him. "I heard. The nurse told me. I was just coming to you now."

"You haven't really ever met her ... the nurse is cleaning her up now—but I know she'll want to meet you. Can you stick around for a bit?"

I hate to burst his bubble, hate to do anything to dampen the smile that stretches across his handsome face. Maybe I should wait. Let him enjoy her survival a little bit longer. But I don't. I'm too much of a busybody—too much of a meddler to let this go. "You need to tell her, Paul. About you and Stewart."

He scowls, the look instantly taking me back in time. Him, six years old, mad over a broken toy. Him, eleven years old, when I refused to let him surf in a storm. "Stewart's gone. Why does it matter?"

"Stewart will never be gone, Paul. He's your brother. She needs to know that—needs to have all the facts so that she understands the situation and makes the right decision."

"Decision?" There is panic in his eyes for a moment. "You told me yesterday Stewart was stepping back. Letting her go. She loves *me*."

"You can't start a relationship with a secret. Let me talk to her. Explain everything. Allow her to come to grips with it."

He leaned against the wall, his features tight. "I don't want to lose her, D."

I nod. "I know."

"She'll choose me, right?"

I meet his uncertain gaze. "I don't know her, Paul. But I know you both. And Stewart isn't at a place in his life where he can fully commit to a relationship. I'm sure she knows that."

His face darkened. "I don't want her to choose me because she can't have him. I want her to choose me because I am who she wants. That's what's important, her happiness."

I squeeze his arm. "Let me talk to her. The 'brother' thing is going to be a lot for her to take. Go get some breakfast."

He doesn't move, staring straight ahead, a lost look on his face, and I leave him there, my heels clicking on the linoleum floor, my mind sorting through how to break this news to a stranger.

MADISON

The nurse pats my arm with a smile, her gray eyes warm and friendly. "I'll be back in an hour to check on you. Page me if you feel any pain."

"When can I go home?" My throat still is on fire, the words coming out scratchy and raw.

She wrinkles her brow. "Probably tomorrow, but the doc will have my hide if she knows I told you that. Let her tell you."

"I feel fine now." It's a lie. My head is killing me, I feel bouts of nausea, and every breath feels like I'm rubbing sandpaper down my throat, but I am ready to leave. I've only been conscious for an hour, and I'm already sick of this place. I want my bed, the sound of waves, and the smell of salt air. Paul's arms around me, his breath on my skin, a warm mug of his lemon tea.

"We still need to monitor you for a while. You've pulled out strong, but with the brain ... nothing is certain." Her smile softens her words, and she grabs my chart and heads for the door, maneuvering around someone as she exits. I look up, expecting Paul, and am surprised by the tall woman who enters, dressed in a black suit, her stern outfit out of place in this world of white. She moves confidently into the room, her eyes on mine, and extends an arm, my own raising out of habit, shaking her hand as I wonder who she is. An insurance rep? Hospital administrator? Her face is familiar, and I study it, trying to place where I have seen her.

"I apologize for coming in so early, but I wanted to introduce myself. My name is Dana. I'm Paul's sister."

I blink at her, our hands still clasped, the handshake reaching an awkward length of time. She releases it and sits in the chair closest to the bed, my mind playing a frantic game of catch-up, ignoring her familiar features while trying to process her words. Sister?

I swallow painfully, my mind piecing together what I know from the little Paul has shared about his past. "Sister? I thought that ..."

She grimaces, her expression pained. "You're thinking of Jennifer. She passed away when Paul was a teenager."

"A car accident."

"Yes. I'm his older sister. I was at college when that happened. Paul probably hasn't mentioned me—he cut all contact with the family when she died."

I nod, a faint recollection of a second sister entering my head. Paul has always been so dismissive in discussing his family, the still-raw pain of his sister's death causing some degree of anger, his reason for the separation from his family not given. It is the one area of his life we don't discuss, the topic a touchy one that turns my cheerful love into a brooding, depressed man. Early in our relationship I pushed the issue, thinking he needed to talk about it. But it put him in such a dark place that, ever since then, I have avoided the subject.

"Is Paul aware that you're here?" I ask carefully, trying to understand her presence.

"Yes, I was here last night." She smiles. "We've reconnected, something I am grateful to you for." Her face pales, and she covers her mouth. "That sounds horrible—I didn't mean—"

I wave her off with a weak smile. "I understood what you meant. I'm glad that you are on good terms again. Family is important."

Her face stills, and she squares her shoulders. "Yes. And *that* is why I wanted to speak to you. Alone, I mean."

I tense, the look on her face, the stiffness of her body. Something is coming, from a stranger whose name Paul hasn't even mentioned in the last two years. I suddenly wish I had pressed him harder over the reason for their strife.

She doesn't mince words or cushion the situation. "I am the oldest of three. Paul is my youngest brother. Stewart—*your* Stewart—is my other brother. Paul and Stewart are brothers … but have been estranged."

I watch her eyes, note that they are brown, not the brilliant blue of my boys. My brain, still sluggish, wonders where the brown came from, if it was the paternal or maternal gene that produced that color. If Paul and my babies would be icy blue or chocolate brown-eyed. Her eyes sharpen, look at me critically, and I realize she is waiting for something. A reaction. I flip back through her words, piecing the sentences together, the structure unnecessarily complicated, the final words suddenly sharpening into focus, my brain comprehending the situation in one, delayed moment. Brothers.

I control my features, my words carefully chosen as my mind tries to figure out the proper response, tries to figure out what this woman wants me to say. I have no articulate response.

I am in love with brothers. My unwinnable situation is more fucked up than original perception would lead you to believe. I still love them just as much, my attraction almost more understandable now that the reasons for their similarities are known. I swallow, and try to speak, try to say something that this woman will respect.

"What do you suggest I do?"

It wasn't the reaction she expects, her visible reaction one of surprise. "Me? I'm not involved in your relationships. I just wanted you to know the reason ... Stewart—"

"... is leaving me." I finish the sentence for her, lying back onto the bed, looking up at the ceiling. It's not a surprise. Circumstances dictated him to choose between a full-time relationship and a full-time commitment to work, and work won. It is his obsession, his passion. I was his release, his outlet. I know he loves me. I never doubted that fact. And I was okay being second, because I had Paul. Paul, who has never placed anything before me. Paul, who would put down his surfboard in a moment if I asked him. And I wonder, briefly, if Paul played a role in Stewart's decision to walk away. If I lost purely to his drive, or if his family was also a factor. And I hope, for whatever reason, that Paul was part of the reason that Stewart backed off.

"Yes. It's not that he doesn't care for you—"

I turn to her, stopping her rushed words, her worried eyes. "I know. You don't have to explain. Stewart's work is who he is. Paul being brought into the situation makes the decision easy for him."

She looks at me carefully. I can see the confusion in her eyes. "So ... you're fine with this."

I swallow, folding over the hem of the blanket. "This situation ... it's always had an end date. In a way I've been preparing for this for a long time. The fact that they're brothers ..." My voice fails for a moment, the rasp too strong, and I reach for the glass of water, taking a sip before continuing. "Stewart's relationship with Paul is more important. Have they spoken?"

She nods. "They haven't reconciled, but I think it is possible. They've both held a lot of anger toward each other for the last ten years, and I think this situation ... it's caused them to let that go. Not that Stewart really has time for family, but ..." She smiles. "Paul is feeling very grateful to Stewart right now."

"For me."

"Yes." She looks at me head-on, with the same direct stare that Stewart uses, one that seems to peer into my soul and strangle the truth from me. "Is that who *you* want? Paul?"

I sigh. "I've asked myself for two years which one of them I would choose—if put in that situation. I love Paul. I love our life together. We fit ... in a way that is easy. Seamless. Stewart is the opposite of me. He gives me a different side to life. I will miss that part; I will miss his intensity, his fire. But just because I'll miss it doesn't mean it is meant to be my everyday. I don't know if I could handle him every day. And I would never be happy with being second to his work. And I could never ask him to work less. You know him. His work … it is his breath. He has a fire for it, it is what makes him tick." I fidget with my hands. "I don't know if I would have ever willingly walked away from Stewart—but this is what's best. I know that. I love Paul. It wasn't really ever fair for any of us—what was going on." I blink, realizing suddenly that tears are welling, embarrassment seeping through me at the weakness. I wipe at my eyes, avoiding her gaze. "I just want him to be happy," I whisper. "I hate the thought of him being alone."

I feel her arms, they wrap around me, the strength of them comforting. And I relax in her embrace and let the tears, and the guilt, flow.

Stewart never came back to the hospital. Every time the door opened, or I heard a voice in the hall, I expected it to be him. But he never returned.

They release me three days later, when I finally reach a point of bitchiness, trying to rip the IV from my arm and biting the heads off anyone but Paul or Dana.

Dana. I finally realize where I know her from, her face turning bright red when I bring it up. It is then, over hospital Jello and shit coffee, that she tells me. How she watched me. Suspected me of some master plan, one that would destroy her brothers. How she hated me from afar. She apologizes, though none is needed, and we hug. And she pays me the nicest compliment I have ever gotten.

"I see why they love you. It is hard, while in your presence, not to love you."

I blush, taking a sip of coffee to disguise the reaction, and think about how vile I have been since waking up chained to this bed. How she is able to see any redeeming qualities is a shock.

Then, finally, they put me in a wheelchair and take me out, Paul's Jeep parked at the curb. The wheelchair is unnecessary; I could have cartwheeled out of there. But some hospital policy requires it, and I am only too happy to oblige.

Anything to speed my exit. Anything to get me out of the sterile environment and back into beach air and sun.

Paul lifts me from the chair despite my protests, taking advantage of the act and brushing his lips over mine, his eyes examining me, filled with emotion. "I love you, Maddy."

I grin at him. "I love you, too."

"I'm so happy you are coming home."

I don't know if he is referring to my near-death experience, or the fact that I am now fully his, without a second man hovering over our relationship. But either way, I am happy, too. More than happy, I am anxious, ready, for our new life together. And yet, there it is. Guilt. Leaning onto my shoulder, whispering in my ear. Every smile, every burst of happiness accompanied by a twinge of guilt. I am coming home to Paul; I am making a life with him. And Stewart will be alone. *Twinge.*

Paul sets me into the front seat and buckles the belt around me, his normal scent—one of ocean and sunscreen—gone. Replaced by hand sanitizer and ivory soap. I'm suddenly anxious for us to swim. To wash away all of the last four days and literally dive back into our old world.

"Paul," I say softly, his head turning quickly at the words.

"Yes, baby? What is it, are you in pain?" His eyes are concerned, and I smile to appease his worry.

"No. When we get home … I want to go in the water. Just for a quick swim."

He studies my face, leaning forward to give me another kiss. "If that's what you want, baby. I'll do anything you want."

Anything. It is true. The last two years have taught me that. *Anything.* It is a heavy word when used correctly. It is a word that can hold unknown possibilities.

It is good to be back. To step from the jeep and walk, my weight gingerly, then confidently, held by my legs. I stretch in our carport before turning to Paul, seeing him round the jeep, his eyes on me, intent, looking for some sign of physical weakness. I grin, shooting him a look he knows, a look that leads to ditched clothes and feverous hands. He returns the smile, relief crossing his features, and reaches for me.

I dip around his hands, dropping my bag on the concrete, and dart into the sunshine outside our garage, surprising him with my speed. "Uh-uh," I click my tongue at him. "Ocean—now."

"I want *you*, now," he growls, stepping out of the darkness, his hand catching my sundress and tugging on the fabric until I am against him. "Seeing as you seem to be back to normal."

I push against him, breaking free and move, grabbing his hand and tugging him along the alley. "First, the water."

He wraps an arm around my neck, pulling me against him and pressing soft kisses on my head as we walk down a broken sidewalk we have traveled countless times before. A block from the water, when we round a corner and see the glint of afternoon sun reflecting off the waves, he bends, catching me off guard, and swoops me into his arms, smiling down at me as he moves.

"It's cold out," he warns. "Are you sure you're up for it?"

"Don't chicken out on me now," I fire back, the sentence causing him to laugh. That beautiful sound, that huge smile I have missed; the closer we step to the water, the less intensity his eyes carry. He pulls me to him for a kiss, then throws me over his shoulder and breaks into a run. I bounce, holding on tightly, and laugh, feeling the change in his stride when his feet reach the sand. I brace for the water.

Freezing, *shockthebreathoutofyou*, cold. Paul hits it first, gasping, then moves in deeper and unceremoniously dumps me into the ocean. His hands pull me to him, my legs instinctively wrapping around his waist and squeezing, seeking the warmth of his body as I move closer.

"Told ya," he whispers, his hands on my skin, rubbing it, warming it slightly as he gathers me against his chest and takes us deeper, the water now at our shoulders, waves rocking us every few moments.

"It is pretty cold," I agree, the click of my chattering teeth causing us to laugh.

He kisses me into silence, sliding his hands under my floating dress, pulling my hips hard into him. "What do you say you let me take you inside? Let the shower warm us up?"

"Or something else," I whisper against his mouth.

"Or something else." He grins, and I squeeze with my legs.

My wet dress feels like an ice pack by the time we stumble, shivering, up the steps to our home. The house is just as I remember it, and I feel a burst of shock at how much has changed since I last walked through these doors.

"Come here," he whispers, adjusting the thermostat, leading me into our bedroom and pulling me close, rubbing his hands over my arms, stealing a quick kiss as he yanks at his shorts and drops them to the floor.

Wow. Anyone who thinks water causes shrinkage has never met this man. At least, not this man at this moment in time. He is, despite the smile he shoots me, raring to go, and I am suddenly warm, my skin tingling, the heat between us erasing anything else.

"Turn around, baby." His words are soft, but I hear their directive and meet his eyes, a curl of pleasure shooting through me at the look in them. Raw need. A fire burning behind his cocky smile. This is the Paul I know, the one who expresses love best through touch, and who can barely contain his emotions in this moment.

I turn, hearing him blow into his hands, feeling the warmth of his skin as he pulls at my dress, his hands gently lifting the wet material off, his fingers lingering on me as they trail down my arm, as if they want every bit of me they can get. A hand tugs at my zipper, pulling it slowly down, his hot breath on my neck as he exhales against my skin, planting a soft wet kiss there, my panties the next victims to his sure and unhurried movement.

He stays close to me, unclasping my bra, his hands sliding down my back and then curving around my sides, slipping under my limp bra and cupping my cold breasts, squeezing them, pulling my body back against his chest, the hot line of his arousal hitting the top of my ass, hot to cold, my body greedy for more contact against his skin. He kisses my neck from behind, whispering my name as his hands explore my front, running over the lines of my stomach, the curve of my breasts, the hard tips of my nipples. I am suddenly needy for him in ways I have never been, needing to know that this is real, that he is mine, and we have made it through this experience intact, the proof of it hard against my backside, and I want it, him, now, in every way that I can have him. His touch slides lower, and I moan, pushing my ass back against him as his hands gently cup me, his mouth taking a delicious line across the hollows of my neck.

"Madd, I never … you have no idea how much I love you," he groans, grinding against me, his hands holding me in place as he pushes the hard ridge of himself antagonizingly close to where I need it.

"Please," I whisper. "Paul, I need to feel it. I need you inside of me."

"In a minute, baby." Instead, I feel his fingers, their gentle exploration over and across my sex, and I push against him, groaning when they finally move inside, slowly sliding in and out, their maddening length and width not enough for what I need.

I moan, my legs weakening from the delicious touch. "Please," I beg.

He rasps, his voice thick at the nape of my neck, his arm wrapping around and hugging me to his chest. "Tell me, Madd. Tell me that you need my cock."

"I do," I pant. "I do. Please. Give it to me." My legs buckle as he crooks his fingers, brushing them back and forth over my pleasure spot.

"Only me," he says firmly, brushing his digits in a way that makes me moan. "Come to the thought of my cock," he whispers. "Then I'll show you exactly what it can do."

I do. I push every lingering thought of Stewart out of my head, physically feel as they leave my body, and focus on Paul—my love—focus on the stiff head of him that is sliding between my legs, inches from where I need it most, so hard that it is sticking straight out. I close my eyes and think about every time he has made me moan, how his face looks when he loses control, the fire in his eyes when he watches me come. The images take me ...

over the edge ...
back arching ...
stars forming ...
pleasure ripping tingling paths through my body ...

Paul's fingers keep up the rhythm, the perfect pressure and tickle across my g-spot, every swipe bringing new life into my orgasm, until I finally sink, held up only by his hands, and look over my shoulder, into his eyes, my drugged vision putting him in a haze, a haze of gorgeous blue eyes and five o'clock shadows.

"Fuck me," I croak, and his eyes darken, a devious smile of carnal possibilities sweeping across his gorgeous face.

"Yes, ma'am."

He pulls me to my feet, making sure I am steady before releasing me. I start to turn, to face him, but he stops my movement. "Face forward. Grab the foot of the bed."

I obey, placing my hands on the footer and arching my back, pushing my ass out and waiting, the heater blowing warm air against my skin, my nipples hardening, my legs clenching. He runs a finger over my sex, dipping inside and then continuing up, until he reaches the tight pucker of my ass, circling the spot. Tight, hard circles, pressing against the hole until I moan, the spot resisting, too tight to allow him entrance. "Please, Paul ... I need you."

His finger moves, sliding back down, taking the temperature of my sex once again, hot wetness confirming my arousal, dragging that liquid higher, soaking my asshole, his thumb replacing the finger, a bigger, harder push, not yet inside, but enough to make my breath catch in my throat.

"Tell me," he says softly, each word feathery gruff, his thumb pushing harder, breaking the seal and entering my darkest place. "Tell me how you want it."

"Hard," I whisper, my senses on full alert, wanting, waiting for what is coming, all of my arousal knotting and expanding from the intrusion in my ass. He pushes harder, deeper inside me—a gasp, followed by a moan, spilling out of my mouth. I grip the footboard tightly, feeling the collection and drip of moisture in my pussy.

"Are you mine?" His voice is tight, guttural, and I smile despite myself, waiting, tense and excited, and coming apart when I feel the width of him, pressing against me, teasing the opening of my body.

"Answer me," his hoarse voice demands, and I hear the raw edge of desperation, his need for confirmation as great as the throbbing in my core. His thumb moves slightly, pushing and then pulling, the hard sting of his hand taking me closer and closer as his finger continues its wet exploration, heat building in my ass, my mind becoming delirious from the sensation.

"All yours, Paul. There is no one else. I—oh God—love you." The words tear from my mouth, my pussy clenching as my ass contracts, every muscle on high alert, loving the feel of his hand as he squeezes and grips my ass.

"God, you are beautiful," he bites out, sliding his fingers into me, dipping them in and out, giving me two, then three fingers, my core tightening around him, prompting a groan to leave his mouth. "Are you ready for me, Madd?"

"Now," I blurt out, the orgasm close, pleasure rolling toward the waterfall edge that will be my flight. "Please, I need you." It is coming, a giant black hole of pleasure and his thumb pushes deeper, the dirty feel of him there so wretchedly hot, pleasure sensors go off around every inch of his thumb, his wet erection hard against my skin, his fingers sliding further, deeper and deeper, slight pain mixing with pleasure, dominance with love. I tilt back my head, *can't hold it any longer*, any coherent thought dropping off as I dive off the edge, into my orgasm, into a perfect black sea that grips my entire body and explodes it into a thousand shards of pleasure.

It is then, while my world caves in, while I am mindlessly oblivious to anything but my own ecstasy, that he shoves fully inside of me.

Fullness. The long, hard ridge of him inside me, branding me as his own, his need as desperate as mine. One hand still on my ass, his thumb making the tight fit of his cock even tighter, his other hand gripping my waist, holding me firm and letting loose on my body with his cock. He doesn't ease into the rhythm, doesn't give either of us time to react. He just dominates me: hard, firm fucks that bury inside with every stroke, a furious rhythm of domination, his breath fast and loud, my name ripping from his lips as he takes me as his own.

We are one combined machine, pistons pumping, lubed and swift, perfectly fitting as it should, no pause in our movements, no hitch in our step. He works his thumb in my ass, pushing and pulling, the tight fit glorious in its intensity. I am going to come again, the shaking of my body, the feel of two holes filled, the animalistic fever of Paul, a man unleashed, the level of his possession so fucking hot.

"Tell me, Madd," he gasps, the hand at my waist sliding down, gripping the sore skin of my ass and forcing me on and off his cock. "Tell me that you are mine."

I can't. I can't respond because my eyes are too tightly shut, my body racking underneath him, pushing harder, greedier against his skin, needing every stroke, every fuck, every inch of his thick cock as I come, a bundling outpour of muscles flexing and contracting, a scream coming from my throat, his hands loosening as I release the sound, my body growing rigid, his fucks continuing, his own climax close.

When I come up for air, I tell him. I tell him how I have always loved him. How he has always had my heart. How now, he will be the only one in it. I look over my shoulder at him, at his beautiful face, hair mussed, eyes vulnerable as he meets my eyes, relief spilling into those blue depths of perfection. He suddenly slows his strokes, the moment changing, and rolls me over, pulling out long enough to lift me onto the bed and settle down above me. He takes my mouth, kissing me deeply, murmuring soft words of love as he spreads my legs with his knees, and enters me again, slower this time, fully thrusting in and then pulling out, his eyes on mine.

It feels so different without Stewart. It feels, in ways, like the first time we've ever made love, like every other time was a threesome with an invisible presence watching over us. Now, as I wrap my legs around his waist, as he leans down and kisses my lips, I feel his relief. I feel an absence of fear, and I realize how unfair I have been to him. I realize how every experience must have seemed a competition, every visit I took to Hollywood prompting worry in him that I might not return. His touch on my skin is now shaky, as if he is unsure I am really here, that it is really true, as if he has to verify it for himself.

I pull him to me, wrap my hands around his neck, lift my mouth to his. And I tell him, in between kisses, how deeply I love him. How I will never leave. How I am his for as long as he will have me.

His breathing slows, his kisses deepen, then he closes his eyes, thrusts deep, and comes.

VENICE BEACH, CA

The effects of drowning are not long-term. Head injury is a fickle bitch; it can sneak back up and knock you on your ass when you least expect it. But there is no reason for bed rest. No reason that Paul has taken a month off surfing to wait on me hand and foot. But I'm not going to complain. I want the worry to fade from his eyes. To him, my death is still too real of a possibility. Time will be the only thing to disquiet his concern.

We sit on the couch, my feet in his hands, his gentle touch rubbing lines in my soles, and it takes a moment to react when my cell rings. I glance at the display, my chest tightening when I see Stewart's name. I changed his contact name the day I returned home, the act of deleting LOVER and replacing it with his name cathartic in its transformation.

I wasn't sure if he'd call. Part of me has feared he'd drop in, every car engine causing my muscles to tighten with nerves. I show Paul the screen, and he squeezes my feet, moving them off his lap, and stands, bending over quickly and dropping a kiss on my cheek. "I'll run out, grab groceries, let you talk." There is a moment when our eyes meet, when unsaid communication flows through them, and I thank God that I know him so well. It is all there, in the slight tightening of his shoulders, in his quick and easy smile that hides so much. *Talk to him. Make sure you are making the right decision. Come back to me. I need you. I love you. I am better for you.*

I reassure him with my eyes, then answer the phone, hearing the jingle of keys and then the firm, complete shut of the door. *Come back to me.*

"Hey babe." The voice is Stewart's—the strain in his words that of a stranger.

I wet my lips and speak, my raw throat abandoning me, my own words scratchy and weak. "Hey."

"I'm sorry I never saw you at the hospital. I was there—until you stabilized. I just, Paul ..." He exhales a loud breath, and I can picture him at his desk, work stacked around him, his hand working through his hair as he flexes his handsome jaw. "The whole thing caught me so off guard. I should have stayed—"

"You did the right thing." He did. I don't know what I would have done if they had both hovered over me. Pulled me in between their hearts, fought over me.

"I love you. You know that."

I feel the sudden urge to cry. Feel the push of emotion in my throat, surging up, and know that the next breath will be a gasp. A shuddering, wet, yes-I'm-crying gasp. I cover the mouthpiece and pull a pillow to my lips, choke back a sob against the yellow cotton. I realize that I have said nothing. That he is waiting, his declaration hanging out there, nothing but silence in response.

"I just feel …" There is a voice in background, then muffled sounds, the scratchy thud of skin against the mouthpiece, and I blink back tears as I hear bits of a very familiar conversation. And I know, before he even returns to the phone, what his next words will be. *I just feel …* Do I even want to know the rest of that sentence? Do I want to know how he feels? Or will it be the final tear that rips my barely-held-together heart?

"Madison, I'm sorry. I—"

"… have to go." I whisper the words, feeling the drip of undeserved tears down my cheeks. I clear my throat, needing to say something before he leaves, hoping he will wait long enough to hear them. "Stewart—one last thing." One last thing. Three casual words that suddenly scream of finality. One. Last. Thing. I swallow the weakness and strive for a clear tone. "I've loved Paul for a long time. I think … we would have ended up here anyway." *I choose Paul.* "You leaving the hospital, you giving us this opportunity …" I clear my throat. "Thank you."

"If you change your mind—I'm here. You know that."

"I know," I say softly. *No, you're not there. Pieces of you not consumed by work are there. You have never been there.*

There is a moment of silence, and then he hangs up the phone. I lean back in, hug the pillow to my chest, and let out the sob.

HOLLYWOOD, CA

STEWART

I take my hand off the phone's hook, the receiver still against my ear, and listen to the drone of the dial tone, my thoughts somewhere else, my mind shaky from the sound of her voice. The door to the office flies open, and Ashley's frame barges in.

"We need you *now*, Mr. Brand. Conference Room Four. Everyone is waiting."

I lift the receiver from my ear, waving a hand dismissively at her, and set it in the cradle. "No need for that. She's gone."

She comes to a stop, her eyes on mine, and her voice drops in pitch and volume. "Are you okay?"

I sigh, the thick exhale rumbling through my throat and run my hand slowly over the top of the desk, feeling the grain of wood beneath my fingers. "I—" the words drop, and I clear my throat, start again. "I fear I have made a mistake."

She takes a moment, sits on the arm of a chair. "Why did you have me cut off the call? Why didn't you talk to her longer?"

I look up, into her eyes, appreciating the frank directness of her stare. "Honestly? I was worried of what I might say."

"You walk away from big deals all of the time."

"She's not a deal." The words roll harshly off my tongue, and she meets my glare without hesitation.

"That's how you treated her, Stewart. And why she never committed to you. You didn't *just* make this decision. You've made it every day I've worked for you. You're right. You have made a mistake. But it wasn't a week ago. It was two years ago. Celebrate that you've finally walked away from it." She stands, her eyes flashing, and sets the folder she carried on the desk. "And my second interruption wasn't an act. You have people waiting in the conference room."

I sits back in my chair, hearing the slam of the door, the irritated clip of her heels fading down the hall. I close my eyes and think of Madison, her grin in the dark of my bedroom. Her hands tugging me closer. The way her laugh releases the tension in my chest.

There, alone in my office, the cold breeze of the air conditioner against my skin, I take a moment and mourn my mistakes.

SMUGGLING: [VERB]
TO HIDE AROUSAL, USUALLY BY
HOLDING YOUR BOARD IN FRONT
OF YOU WHILE WALKING.

There are ways you shouldn't think about your future brother-in-law. Places that should be off-limits for your mind to wander. Like right now. I am watching him, his hand skimming down the open back of her dress, slipping inside and gripping her waist, his thumb rubbing a soft pattern on her skin. My eyes cannot pull from that spot, from the slow motion of his hand, the seductive pass over her skin. I know how that feels, know how frantic he gets when he fucks, how he pushes deep with his cock, pins you to the mattress, or the desk, or the floor, his hands hard on your wrists, his face intense above you, heat and raw need in his eyes. I blink, turning away, stepping to the kitchen, and look for Dana. Her strength grounds me; her knowledge of everything we have been through reassures me.

She smiles at my entrance, waving me over with a flour-covered hand. "I need those fingers. Come knead this dough."

I wash my hands in the small island sink and pat them dry on a hand towel, joining her at the counter, my hands diving into the sticky dough, grateful for the job.

"How's it going?" she murmurs.

"Fine." I say softly, though no one is close enough to hear. "I've only spoken to him once—when he introduced me to her."

"And ..." She reaches for flour, sprinkles a line of it on the counter. "What do you think of her?"

I think about the question, how to word my response. "I think ..." I pause to scratch my hairline with my forearm. "That she is nice. Accommodating. Stewart says she's a web designer?"

She snorts. "That's putting it lightly. She created a music-sharing site that just signed a deal with Apple."

So the bubbly blonde with the sparkling smile is successful. Intelligent. I wait for the flow of jealousy that should come, should poke its green head up, but instead, a smile forms. I've spent so much of the last year feeling guilty. My life with Paul has been wonderful—perfect. But every bit of happiness felt slightly tainted by the fact that Stewart was alone, left out in the cold as Paul and I continued full-steam ahead in our happy relationship. And now, with our engagement, I've been terrified of how Stewart will react. How the brothers' new, fragile relationship will weather the announcement. To see Stewart happy, with a girl who surpasses me ... it lifts that guilt, sends a spike of relief through me. He will be okay. We will be okay. I can continue with my new life—guilt-free.

That doesn't stop the attraction. Our entire relationship was built on sex. Hot, fuck-my-panties-to-pieces sex. It was how we connected, communicated. It will be strange to move into a cordial relationship. One where we chat about life and friendship, and if the Dodgers will beat the Giants.

I feel arms slip around me, gripping my waist and pulling me tightly against hard muscle, a soft kiss nuzzled into the crook of my neck, and a giggle bursts from my throat as I hold up dough-covered hands. "Stop," I gasp. "The bread!"

"The bread can wait," Paul says softly, spinning me around, his mouth taking mine, a soft kiss that presses back my head and deepens into something more, his pelvis dipping into me, my belly curling at the contact. I moan against his mouth.

"Wow." The wry voice is really, really close. So close that I open my eyes in surprise, Dana's half-smile only steps away. "Point made. You guys can heat each other's clothes off. I got two bedrooms upstairs should you feel the need for more." She stares pointedly at Paul. "Now 'git, loverboy. Go back and tend to the steaks and let me have some time with her."

He grins at her, lifting me without warning, his hands strong on my waist, setting me on the edge of the counter and taking one last kiss. "I love you, baby."

"I love you, too," I whisper, glancing around quickly before shooing him away. "Now go, before Stewart comes back."

"He's too gaga over Website Barbie to notice," he says happily, his relief matching my own. "He already invited us to join them in San Francisco next weekend."

I frown. "San Francisco?" Stewart, taking a weekend off? That doesn't sound anything like the man I know—knew.

Dana barrels through, shoving Paul aside, his wink disappearing in a blur of brunette dominance. "That's it. Outside. You get all damn night with her. Give me a measly fifteen minutes." She points to the back door, her expression firm, and he backs up, hands up, sending me a playful smile before heading outside.

She shoots me an exasperated look. "Please tell me he's not like that all the time."

I bite back a smile. "Okay."

She pulls out a pan and unwraps a stick of butter, spreading it around the base.

"So ... you hiding that ring for a reason?"

I glance toward the living room, the muted voices alerting me of Stewart's presence. "You know why. I'm going to tell him tonight, but I want to do it privately."

She stares me down until I met her eyes. "You scared?"

"I'm ... nervous. It'll be our first real conversation—in person at least—since the accident. It helps that she's here. That he's happy. Paul wanted to tell him, but this is important to me. I think we need this conversation."

She nodded. "I agree. It was one of the reasons I invited everyone over. That, and I've been itching for a family Thanksgiving since I bought this house." She grins. "No other point in having a twelve-person dining room set."

I try to return the smile, but my stomach is suddenly in knots, the reminder of my impending news sobering.

The Thanksgiving meal is a success, the table filled with turkey, ham, and enough side items to feed a family three times our size. We eat our fill, and then move, leaving the dishes, the boys sprawling out on leather sofas in the den, football suddenly on the television. I stand in the doorway and watch Stewart for a moment before entering. Football. I've never known Stewart to have time for sports, save reading scores and standings while hurrying through the news. His arm is around her, her blonde hair against his sweater, her feet tucked underneath a thick blanket of Dana's. I tap his shoulder gently, the contact causing him to jump silently, and his head whips around to look up at me.

"Could I speak to you for a minute?" I smile awkwardly at Mia. "I won't keep him long, I promise."

He squeezes her shoulder, placing a quick kiss on her head. "I'll be right back, babe." She smiles sunnily, turning back to the game, and responds to an insult Paul had just flung out to the television. She is so comfortable, with Paul, with Stewart, and I marvel at her easy fit into the strange dynamic that we make. Paul and Stewart have seamlessly slid back into old roles, their love apparent throughout dinner, jabs and insults exchanged as easily as compliments. I am the one at odds, my stiffness with Stewart causing a hitch in this renovated machine. I hope this conversation helps.

He holds open the door for me, and we step outside, my skin standing at attention in the cool fall air. I shiver slightly, and his eyes sharpen on the movement, his movement visibly restrained when he starts to move forward and stops. We both laugh awkwardly. "Want to sit on the steps?" he offers.

"That sounds great."

We sit, his long legs stretching down the steps, and he turns, facing me, his eyes close on and moving over my face, as if he is memorizing the features. "I've missed you."

My eyes close, blocking out the view of his concern. I hesitate over the words, and then let them free. "I've missed you, too. We had some good times."

He chuckles. "Yeah. Most of our good times involved very little clothing."

Color floods my cheeks, and a grin breaks out at the truth in his statement. "Yeah."

"I'm sorry I didn't call again. To follow up, after the accident." His voice is so somber I look up to find his eyes on me, serious and dark.

I frown, confused. "You had work. You always have work. I understood that—that's how your life is."

"Was," he corrects me gently. "I'm trying to be different with Mia. Something Dana said—after the accident—stuck with me. With her, it's not the same—I'm putting aside work more, making time for her." He looks apologetic as he speaks, and I smile at him.

"I'm glad, Stewart. I'm glad you have someone who you care enough about to do that." I stutter, realizing how the words sounded. "I … I mean—I'm happy for you."

"I'll always love you, Madison," he says quietly, my heart tugging at the words, his eyes on mine. "I love you for mending this family—for letting me see what is possible—for making Paul happy. But the 'in love' with you part … I've moved on from that. I'm really happy for you. For both of you."

I blink back the tears that have found their way to my eyes. In a way, it is heartbreaking. I'm looking at the man I always hoped Stewart would become. A man who would spend Thanksgiving with family, who would sit on the couch and not look at his phone. A man who realized what was important, and who had found someone he loved enough to adjust his life for. Someone who wasn't me. I've never been so happy to be so easily replaced. "Working less, huh?" I choke out a laugh. "That makes me really happy for you, Stewart.

He reaches his arm out, wrapping it around my shoulders and squeezing me to his side. "We're gonna be okay, right?"

"We better be." I grin. "We're gonna be stuck together for a while." I push away enough to look into his eyes. "In fact, that was one of the things I wanted to talk to you about."

He moves a bit on the step so he can face me. "What's wrong? What is it?"

I hesitate. "Nothing's wrong. Paul proposed."

If I have any doubt of Stewart's sincerity, it disappears when the grin splits his face. A *grin*. Stewart ... doesn't really grin. Not normally. He scowls, he glints, but *grinning* ... it is such an odd look that I stare at him in surprise. He grabs my hand, his smile dropping when he sees the bare skin. "You said no?"

I shake my head with a laugh. "No, I accepted. I just didn't want to show up wearing a ring ... without talking to you about it."

He sweeps me into a hug, hugging me tightly, so tightly I squeak.

"You're happy?" I laugh, pushing out of the hug.

"You'll be my sister now, Madison. As totally creepy as that is, seeing as I still got a raging hard on when you walked in the house—"

"Shut up," I choke out, blushing, my own inappropriate thoughts coming to mind.

"Seriously," he says, grabbing my hand. "You'll always be in my life now. That couldn't make me happier. And Paul—he loves you so much. More than I ever did. He deserves you, Madd."

"Madd? You've never called me that before." I wrinkle my nose at him.

He shrugs. "Things are different now."

"So ... we have your blessing?"

He wraps an arm around my neck, pulling, and placing a quick kiss on my forehead. "More than that, babe. More than that. You have my heart. Both of you." He releases me and stands, holding out a hand and helping me up.

"Did he get you a good ring?" he asks gruffly.

I nod with a smile. "He did good. You'd approve." And he *had* done well. It wasn't a Stewart ring, picked out by his assistant, wasn't a huge rock that shouted my status while begging me to be mugged. But for Paul and me, it was perfect. A blue sapphire, the color of the ocean after a storm, tiny diamonds making up the band, leading delicately up to and framing the stone.

Paul designed it, agonized over it, and his eyes were glued to my face when he presented it, early one morning, when I was still half asleep, his proposal coming after coffee, my body wrapped in a big blanket, the ocean air blowing through the open window. He handed me coffee, and I waited for him to join me, to sit behind me and wrap his arms around me, pull me back against his chest. It was how we often spent our mornings, the lazy ones that didn't involve early morning sex or surfing. Instead, he dropped to one knee, his eyes tight to mine, his hands fumbling as he opened the box and extended it. He had choked out the question, his voice tight, his hands shaking, his eyes glued to mine. And I sat there, for one shocked moment, before my mind responded, and I launched myself into his arms, covering him with kisses and whispering the word yes.

He had been worried, nervous. Scared for whatever reason that I would say no. But he had nothing to worry about. I've always been his. I've loved him since the moment I saw his playful grin in a line at Santa Monica Pier, his eyes studying me as I took the place next to him. And finally, with my relationship status one devastating blue-eyed brother less, we had nothing holding us back.

I step into Dana's great room, and watch Stewart pull Paul into a congratulatory hug, their faces holding matching, dimpled grins. I watch them, no sign of tension or competition in the air. It is incredible, that this train wreck ended in such a perfect fashion. My boys, the ones I fought so long to keep separate, embracing. I will get to keep them both in my life. I have emerged with my heart intact. And get to continue life with the man I love. The one who, from the beginning, has waited patiently for this chance.

I cross the room to him, his gorgeous face beaming as he collapses on the couch, pulling me to him, his arm looping around my neck. I lean back into his chest, and look into his eyes.

Their eyes. It should have been my first clue. Piercing blue, too gorgeous, too unique to be a coincidence. But this man's eyes … they see into my soul. They know every bit of me, and accept it all. I will grow old with this man. I will have his babies and teach them to surf. And try, through it all, to be worthy of his love.

EPILOGUE

GLASSY: [ADJECTIVE]
SMOOTH SEAS RESULTING FROM
CALM WIND CONDITIONS, LITTLE DISRUPTION,
NOTHING HIDDEN BENEATH THE SURFACE

I knew. I'd known for a long time. Since I'd opened our mailbox one day and saw Paul's real last name. Not the one he'd used for as long as I'd known him, the one plastered over surfer magazines and endorsement deals. I'd known he used a pseudonym, one for the press, but I had never taken the time to dig deeper. Paul Linx was how I knew him, was how he lived his everyday life. But that day, on the broken concrete that led to our garage, I flipped through envelopes and stopped at one with a different last name. Paul Brand. A unique last name. So unique it made my hand shake, the mail scattering on the ground. I told myself it was probably a coincidence. A crazy, highly unlikely coincidence. As crazy and highly unlikely as dating two men who end up being related.

All of the similarities between them suddenly flooded my mind. Piercing blue eyes. A kissable curved mouth. Rugged features. Tall, athletic builds. Even the impressiveness that hung between their legs. *Jesus.* Both of them, estranged from their families. Both who had—at some point in time—mentioned a brother. I was stupid for not seeing the possibility sooner.

I, scooping up the mail, stumbling upstairs, had full-blown panicked. Sat on the couch, counted to ten, then, twenty, then one hundred, breathing deep, ragged gasps of air, my mind racing with the implications.

At the time, it had seemed disastrous. Insurmountable. Right then, right that moment, I would have to choose. I had to pick. There was no going around it.

But it was too late. My heart had gone too far, jumped over two cliffs and plummeted past the point of return. I could not choose. I could not willingly rip a piece of my heart off and flush it down the toilet. Break up with one of these men with no way to explain the reason. I couldn't. I couldn't throw a bomb into this perfect world where everything was flowing so well, smiles all around, orgasms at every turn.

So I didn't do anything at all. I left the mail on the counter, and went about my life the same as before. But I made sure to keep my lives separate. Made sure to never mention their names or details of our separate lives. Not that the boys cared. They were blissfully ignorant of each other and happy about it. So I lived the life, knowing the entire time there was an expiration date. Knowing that one day the truth would come out and our perfect world would implode.

I dreaded that implosion for so long. Stressed over it, worried over what disasters it would bring. But now? I roll over in bed, burrowing against Paul, who wraps his arms around me, pulling me close, and gently presses his lips to my forehead. I think I knew all along how this would probably end.

Deepak Chopra once said: "All great changes are preceded by chaos." Looking back, chaos was a great way to describe our lives. I saw it as perfection, only because I didn't know what could exist, what lay on the other side. Now? Now that I know? I am grateful for the chaos. Grateful for the immense change that it brought. Grateful that now, I am in a pleasant state of calm.

NOTE FROM THE AUTHOR

WHEW! This book was a rollercoaster to write. I had a huge block about 60% in, when I kept wringing my hands and screaming 'I don't know who to choose!'. Yes, Paul won. Which is funny, because I had always expected her to end up with Stewart. But my characters rarely behave, which is one reason why I love them so much. I would be remiss if I didn't thank a few lovely ladies, who helped shape this book and who gave it the slaps and pinches it needed. First off, my fabulous editor, Madison Seidler – who I fear even mentioning because I'd love to monopolize her lovely self! Thank you for believing in this book, giving it wonderful shape and structure, and for not flinching despite this naughty girl having your own name. Also, Keelie – you are a reading demon and I don't know how you have time to breathe, but I appreciate your advice and friendship and your promotion – you are wonderful! Wendy – you are always available, whenever I shout – thank you for introducing me to so many amazing bookies, and for your insight and direction on this book. I seriously owe you a ginormous hug if I ever make it back to that side of the nation. And Sandra and Elaine – between Goodreads and Twitter, you girls have my back. Thanks for pimping this book and giving me your thoughts, you ladies rock my world.

I do have an *extra special* bonus scene – if you are feeling frisky, please visit http://www.alessandratorre.com/secretfantasy/ - and enjoy!

More Special Thanks to:
Chris at Chris Book Blog Emporium
Angie at Smut Book Club
Shelley & Courtney at MustReadBooksorDie Blog
Mistress L and Mistress M at S&M Book Obsessions
Rose at Rose's Book Blog
Dani & Monique at Just Booked!
Lisa at True Story Book Blog
Nicola at Flirty Dirty Book Blog
Sarah at Books She Reads
And all of the incredible bloggers, readers, and reviewers that I have missed. Please know that – if I have missed your name on this list, you are still dearly loved and appreciated. Thank you so much!

Xoxo,

Alessandra Torre
www.alessandratorre.com

8490885R00155

Printed in Great Britain
by Amazon.co.uk, Ltd.,
Marston Gate.